SOME PEOPLE NEED
KILLING

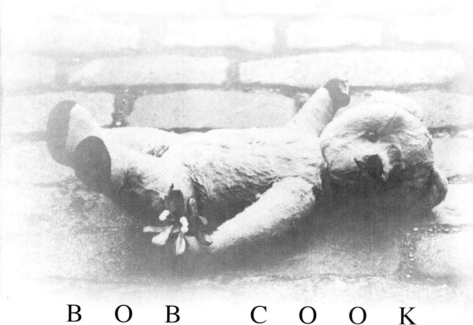

B O B   C O O K

ISBN: 1453734651
ISBN-13: 9781453734650
Library of Congress Control Number: 2010911438

Acknowledgements

In a past life I spent 30 years working with delinquent and dependent children in all levels of responsibility from counselor to administration. We called the line troops halfway house counselors, detention workers, juvenile probation or parole counselors, abuse investigators, foster care or protective services workers, adoption specialists, social workers and so on. These folks weren't perfect. But by and large almost all of them tried their best to turn families around and to stop kids from getting lost before they even got started in life. These people work for low pay and they get scant recognition. But they are out there by the thousands pounding the streets. Here's to you gang. May you have two or three good days this week!

I would like to thank Lt. Steve Ordonia and crime scene investigator Nichole Heintzelman, of the Pensacola Police Department for details concerning police business. I probably don't have it exactly right yet, but without their help, descriptions herein would probably read like the Keystone Cops or something.

I would like to acknowledge the assistance that I receive from a long time friend of my wife, a consummate English teacher, who taught in our gifted programs for decades.

I now consider her my mentor and friend as well. She gave me the courage to tell my stories and now pushes and prods for more in the writing itself.

Finally I must publicly thank my wife for working along side of me. Writing a book is like taking a journey and it is always better to have your best friend by your side to share the adventure as you travel along.

Author's Notes

This novel is a work of fiction. Names, characters, and incidents are the product of the author's imagination and have no relationship whatsoever to anyone bearing the same name or names. All incidents are pure invention. Any references to real events, businesses, schools, organizations, and locales are intended only to give the fiction a sense of reality and authenticity. Any resemblance to actual persons, living or dead, is entirely coincidental.

Chapter 1

"His what?" Beth hollered from down the hall.

"His penis!" Cletus repeated.

"Some jerk is exposing himself to his own child at a house on Jackson. He supposedly just did it a short time ago. It's classified as an immediate investigation. I hate to do this to you, but I need you to roll on this now."

Beth Jacoby sighed audibly but accepted the computer print out from Cletus without complaint. Beth was literally named Prettiest Girl, Class Clown, and Most Likely to Succeed during her senior year in high school. While her face was a little full, she compensated for it by flashing a gorgeous smile and batting baby blue eyes under a thick head of long black, naturally curly hair that was the envy of all the women who knew her. The girl next door in a slim, yet curvaceous body, Beth could disarm anyone because she was intelligent, extremely confident in herself and fully committed to others, qualities that served her well during her four plus years as a child abuse investigator.

Ten lousy minutes, she thought. The report had come in at 4:50 PM. The case would have been assigned to the on-call investigator after 5:00. She was supposed to meet friends for dinner at 6:00. But considering the nature of the report, she tossed her frustration and bolted out the door knowing full well the case had to be investigated ASAP.

She pulled up in front of the house, clearly marked with the address in the report, and parked her fire engine red Mustang behind a rusty dryer that had been pushed into the street. Then she gathered up her notebook while giving the house a quick inspection. It was different than the others on the block. It was large and was at one time the best of the lot. Perhaps it still was. But now it definitely showed its age, its faded, mustard yellow paint reflecting more of a sickly jaundice than fresh sunflower.

The house sported some older gingerbread trimming and a large covered front porch that gave it some charm, the look of a quaint old boarding house. There she spied a young girl looking directly back at her. The kid looked to be about five or six. She was pretty and well dressed in jeans and a nice, pink top, her black hair pulled back in pig-tails. She wondered if the girl was one of the subjects in the report. She got out and climbed the front steps. She had not even reached the porch when the girl spoke.

"Did you come to see Daddy's penis?"

"What?" Beth replied, more to make sure she was hearing correctly than anything else.

"My Daddy's got a big penis. Did you come to see it?"

"Well, in a way," Beth said, now shocked by the nature of that very adult question and the relaxed, friendly nature of the child who was asking it.

"I did come to ask about it," she offered, smiling inwardly at the awkward truth of the matter.

"What's your name, honey?" Beth asked.

"Helen," the little girl said, smiling politely.

Then she asked the child a question that went straight to the reason for her visit.

"Helen, has your father been showing it to you?"

"Why sure. I tried to sneak Lawanda and Saleah in to see it too. But Daddy got really mad. But I think it will be OK if you want to see it. You're grown like my Momma. He's in the front room trying to take a nap."

Wow! This ought to be interesting, Beth thought.

"If it's all right with you, let's go talk to your father."

Without a word, the little girl reached over and grasped Beth's hand, opened the door, and led the investigator into the house. They were just inside when she saw him in a family room off the main hall. The man was sprawled out on a couch wearing only a pair of boxers, struggling to pull a stretched out, white sock over what appeared to be a massive erection which protruded like a pole straight out of his drawers.

"Damn Helen!" he roared. "I told you not to bring those kids around here!"

And then twisting around he quickly noticed that he had serious company. Looking directly at the strange woman in his home with real surprise and a not too subtle hint of frustration on his face, he blurted out "Who in the hell are you?"

"Mr. Carter, Clarence Carter, my name is Elizabeth Jacoby," she said fumbling with her identity card.

"I am a child abuse and neglect investigator from the Department of Children's Services. I am here to investigate a report we received concerning indecent exposure. I assume quite honestly that I have come to the right place."

"Shit!" Mr. Carter managed to get out while yanking up a sheet to cover himself. In the doing, he fluffed it high and let it settle gently onto his swollen member.

Beth was getting furious. How dare the SOB sit around like that exposing himself to his own kid?

She took a deep breath and used a moment to calm herself. She noted that the house was clean and orderly, which reminded her that creeps can and do show up in any household. She was about to speak when the sheet caught her eye.

As it settled and nestled over the man's erect penis, Beth almost laughed out loud. The result of the cover up reminded her of those Halloween ghosts people make with pillowcases, white hankies and such. In this example, the sheet formed a spirit rising up out of the man's body. All it needed was a couple of eyeholes.

But, she recovered quickly to get back to the job at hand. "Care to tell me what you think you are doing here, Mr. Carter?" she asked. "Unfortunately for you I have witnessed the whole thing, so please don't try to give me a line of bull either. Please explain just what are you doing?"

"What are you talking about? Just leave me alone," he said quietly but with a hint of hostility in his voice.

"Listen buster, we can do this the hard way or the easy way," Beth responded.

"Why are you exposing yourself like that?"

"Maryanne!" he screamed. "Maryanne!"

The outburst confused Beth for a second. The thin, handsome black man was glued to the couch and writhing in what appeared to be pain. Or was it pleasure? He made no effort to get up. He seemed to be in some kind of distress. But the erection was just that, a pillar, with no signs of flaccidity. And who was Maryanne?

Suddenly a beautiful young woman hurried into the room. Beth stared at her, thinking she had seen her before, perhaps on television. She was sporting great looking black hair, soft, liquid brown eyes with long, glamorous lashes, and perfect olive skin. She could have been a model.

"Who is this?" she asked, looking from husband to the stranger and back again.

But it was Helen who spoke up first, "Momma, this is Elizabeth. She came to see Daddy's penis."

Beth had forgotten about Helen. For certain, with that particular comment, the child had definitely made her presence known.

There is nothing like the simple truth of a child, Beth thought. But she could have gone all year without the little girl's attempt to help explain her presence. Her response was on the way out of her mouth when Maryanne beat her to the punch.

"What!" the woman thundered. "How dare you walk into our home like this? Who are you anyway? Helen, didn't I tell you? Clarence, who is this woman? Lady you can just turn around and get out of here right now," she said angrily, her head pivoting around rapidly like a weather vane in a storm.

"Lady, if you don't leave my house right now, I'm going to throw you out!"

"Wait!" cried Beth, rather weakly.

And then, recovering, "I'm an investigator with the Florida Department of Children's Services, based here in Pensacola."

"What! You have no business marching into our home. You came to see my husband's penis? How did you know about that anyway? You hear about that from the damn neighbors? Got real nosey and curious, didn't you? Just dropped by to see my husband's manhood? I guess you haven't seen a black man's penis, have you? They are larger than those little pinky fingers white men carry around, aren't they. Well, you aren't getting any of that here, Baby. You can go out and get that on your own!"

"And who gave you permission to talk to my child. I don't care who you are; you have no business around my little girl. You make me sick. If you don't leave right now, I am going to toss you right down the front steps. Do you understand me?"

Beth now realized she had inadvertantly created a very weird ménage a trois. She stood directly in the path of an angry woman who somehow thought she was there to gape at her man. How to get out of this one, she asked herself.

But before she could respond, the little girl spoke up again. "Momma, I didn't talk to her. You told me never to speak to strangers, and I didn't. She just came in the house."

Gee whiz, Beth thought. I understand that the kid is scared because her mother is so angry, but she really isn't helping me here. Then she gathered herself and spoke.

"Mrs. Carter, I am an investigator. I am not a police officer but I have the authority to be here by law and complete an investigation. We have received a report that your husband has been exposing himself to your child. If you try to stop me, the police will be here for sure, but to arrest YOU for obstruction. Now please, let's all settle down. What is going on here?"

"Exposing himself?" the wife shouted, her face now contorted with seething hostility.

"Who told you he was exposing himself? Who told you such a lie as that?"

"Unfortunately Mrs. Carter, I am not at liberty to say," offered Beth.

She hated what she had to say next. It always sent angry people over the top.

"The names of people who make reports are confidential by law. It is done that way to protect the reporter. Otherwise many people would not call the agency and children would be abused and neglected with no way to get help."

"That's just perfect. You stand there and tell me that my husband has been exposing himself and someone reported it but you can't tell me who! That is crazy. I thought this was a free country not Nazi Germany. I am a citizen of this country, and I have rights. Just get out of my house! Leave! Leave before I throw you out!" Maryanne screamed hysterically.

Beth changed her mind about this woman. She really wasn't that pretty after all, particularly as her unfettered rage had contorted her attractive face into a swollen and blotchy mess. The threats did not bother Beth. She was simply not afraid of her would-be attacker. She had grown up the fourth child of six, her siblings being all boys. She was the proverbial tomboy. More to the point, she took up karate, in part because she couldn't play football in school with the guys. Now she was an assistant instructor with a black belt, second degree. But, she prided herself in her ability to handle people without violence. In truth, she had never had to use her skills in earnest. So, she calmed herself, prepared herself, and spoke again.

"Mrs. Carter, forget the reporter. I just saw your husband expose himself to your own daughter."

Maryanne really lost it then. Her eyes bulged and her mouth flew wide-open, spewing spittle as she exploded. "You bitch! How dare you! He has a hard-on! It's nothing but a hard-on! Can't you leave us alone? Just leave us alone."

The outburst seemed to drain the wife. Visibly her whole body sagged, like a sail that had lost the wind. She stood her ground but there were no more threats of violence. She gave an audible sigh, like she was exhausted by it all, glanced aside and pulled out of the fierce eye-to-eye contact she had had with her adversary.

Beth saw the opening and she took it. She lowered her voice and gave it a soft, empathetic tone.

"Mrs. Carter, I will walk out on the porch for awhile to give you some time to think. But I am not leaving. I have no quarrel with you. I just need to get clear on what your husband has been doing," Beth said calmly, hoping to defuse the situation.

But as she turned, Beth's eyes fell on Clarence Carter again. He had discarded the sheet and sock and was lying very still with his eyes closed, his member a lighthouse, a huge phallus, demanding that she stop and, yes, stare.

And she did.

After a moment she caught herself, yanking her head around expecting Mrs. Carter to be on the attack again for gawking at her husband's penis. But Maryanne was standing with her mouth partially open eyeing her husband's protuberance as well. It was, in truth, larger than life and the two women were both fascinated and abhorred by it. Perhaps for the first time, each one came to understand that something was very, very wrong.

"Momma." whispered Helen. "Daddy's crying."

And so he was.

Then it hit her. Beth risked a question that might fuel the fire all over again, but it had to be asked

"Maryanne, is your husband using Viagra or one of those enhancement medicines?" she said calmly.

Beth was a little surprised that Maryanne did not hesitate.

"Why, yes. Yes he is."

Beth then took Maryanne aside, away from the little girl. She needed to know how long it had been since the couple had had intercourse. Maryanne explained that her husband had the afternoon off. He had arrived home around 12:00 P.M.. Helen was in school so they enjoyed some time together. She guessed that it was around 12:30 P.M. that they had had sex. Beth looked at her watch. That was now a little over five hours ago. She advised Mrs. Carter that the drug was probably the problem and that he would no doubt need medical attention.

Beth excused herself and went out to the Mustang. A few neighbors had gathered right in front of the house perhaps attracted by the noises from within. When she made eye contact, they turned, tried to look inconspicuous, and slowly strolled on up the street.

She hopped into the privacy of her car and made a call on her cell phone. The emergency room physician she wanted to talk with was on duty and after awhile he picked up. They talked briefly. Then Beth hurried back into the Carter home. Later, she helped Maryanne load her husband and daughter into their vehicle for a quick trip to the emergency room. Beth followed in the Mustang. As she passed the knot of neighbors who had been trying diligently to get a look at the goings on, she smiled sweetly and waved to them like they were old friends.

When they arrived at the emergency entrance, staff came out and gently placed Mr. Carter on a gurney. Beth looked after the child while Maryanne attended to registration and to her husband. Helen asked one question after another and Beth fielded them as best she could. Basically she explained to the girl that her father had a medical problem that made his penis swell up, and he needed the doctors to make it better.

She also explained to the little girl that, yes, her mother had used a bad word, but didn't mean to do it. She had just been very upset.

She did not tell the little girl that her father needed to be seen by a specialist as soon as possible for treatment of priapism, a persistant erection caused by the lack of blood flow out of the penis following an erection. Beth hardly understood the condition herself and had certainly never come across it before in child welfare. The emergency room physician did tell her that Mr. Carter was lucky she dropped by the house. If his problem had gone on unchecked, he could have become impotent because of tissue damage and experienced other complications.

After what seemed like hours, Clarence Carter was admitted and assigned to a room. A specialist arrived shortly thereafter to begin treatment. Beth stayed with the mother and her child until they finally headed home. As she approached her car to head back to the office, Beth changed her mind. She followed Helen and her mother back to the old yellow house. She wordlessly walked them to the door. There she paused while Maryanne unlocked the door and ushered her child inside. Beth stiff and feeling exhausted was about to turn to leave when Maryanne caught her eyes and mouthed the words, "thank you." Beth acknowledged the message with a nod and a slight smile. As she walked to her car, she enjoyed a renewed sense of energy. By the time she drove off, her tense muscles were beginning to relax, and she was wearing a full grin.

She stopped by a burger joint for a bite to eat, gulping down a grilled chicken sandwich while driving to her office. A night watchman let her in. She found her desk and filed her report, typing rapidly on her computer keyboard. Then she picked up two other cases she had been investigating and brought them up to date as well. Later she drove to her apartment and caught some of the late news on TV before calling it a day.

She would be back in the office before 7:30A.M, primed and ready to roll again.

Chapter 2

Cletus's child abuse investigations unit was one of three such units tasked to investigate all reports of the abuse, neglect, and abandonment of children. They, along with single units for protective in-home supervision, foster care, and adoptions, represented the whole of the state's effort to protect dependent children in Escambia County, Florida. The entire group was housed together in a complex, which also included offices for court personnel, two courtrooms and witness rooms, staff dedicated to delinquency services and other ancillary programs for kids in trouble, dependent, delinquent, runaway, truant and ungovernable.

His current crew, now made up of five investigators and one secretary, gathered around the coffee pot in their pedestrian conference room every morning. Ernie was almost always the first to arrive, spot on at 7:00. This morning was no exception. He made the coffee and had it waiting for the others. He never complained about it either.

Ernie Langhorne mothered and fussed over the unit like it was his family. He, in the role of unit secretary, was a source of comfort and support to everyone in the unit including his supervisor, Cletus Jones. Especially Cletus Jones. Always positive, always upbeat, and never a discouraging word, Ernie charged through each day giving to all that he encountered a full burst of sunshine and fresh air as he breezed through life with an unmistakable, feminine manner, style, and voice.

They all had long since become his friend and greatest ally. Ernie was what he was, an obvious, flamboyant homosexual. His mannerisms were female in nature and his voice occasionally jumped an octave when he became excited. It was rumored that he cross-dressed for fun, but no one really knew much of his private life.

Cletus hired him when no one else would. Cletus, a huge Black man, had played football in college, riding an athletic scholarship from Auburn University all the way to a degree, fulfilling a promise he had made to his grandmother before she died. Perhaps firmly secure with his own masculinity and familiar with the concept of prejudice, he saw nothing to bar him from giving Ernie a chance. Now, no one, not even the judges or the ranking court or law enforcement officials who had occasion to see Ernie in action, dared whisper a disparaging word without risking a serious visit from old number 99 on the program.

In truth, Ernie himself was responsible for his acceptance. Even most of those who honestly condemned homosexuals came to like him and soon forgot that he was one.

Beth Jacoby came in next. She had slept well, rewarded for a long evening with a simple wordless expression of thanks. She was all a glow and on top of her game, ready for the starting bell.

"Wow, look at you, Honey," gushed Ernie as she bolted into view.

"Where did you find that blouse? I believe that the boys will readily see that there is one hot young lady under there."

"Oh Ernie cut the bull, you are embarrassing me," Beth said.

"Why that's a perfectly gorgeous mauve isn't it?" asked Ernie, completely ignoring Beth's objection. "Mauve and black is so sexy!"

"Ernie, please!" Beth sighed.

"I'm sorry, Honey," said Ernie. "You work late again? It's just that you don't notice how the guys check you out when you pass them in the hall. But then again there is always one for me too. You know, between the two of us we drive them ALL crazy, don't we?"

"You are so right, Ernie," said Beth.

"Who's right?" asked Shanice Gooding from the doorway.

"Hey Honey, how are you doing this morning? You sure look great today, pretty girl," said Ernie.

"Ooooh you can talk to me like that all day. Thanks for the compliment," Shanice said, her voice swooning a bit.

"I wish all men were as sweet as you. I can't seem to find a single man who is actually mature enough to love a woman. Every man I meet is little more than a peacock strutting around trying to show off his pretty feathers."

"Come on, Shanice," said Ernie. "You always have men tripping all over themselves to get to you."

"There is a line in Hotel California that I like. It goes something like this. "She has a lot of pretty boys but none of them are men." That's not a direct quote, understand, I changed it a bit. But it sure defines me these days," Shanice said.

A trim Black woman with short-cropped hair, Shanice was stylishly dressed and carried herself with a noticeable combination of grace and great confidence. She had been born into a wealthy family, the father a physician, her mother, an accomplished account executive. She was a fourth generation Floridian. Her great-grandfather was one of the very first black men to open a successful business in Pensacola after the Civil War. He was a cobbler, originally from Philadelphia and specialized in making fine leather boots. His many descendants referred to him proudly as the Damn Yankee or the Carpetbagger.

Shanice was raised to believe that she could do anything she wanted. With a keen mind and connections, she could have followed almost any career track. But what did interest her was the plight of abused children. She chose to enter that little unit meeting room where her colleagues gathered instead of an elegant boardroom in a bank or law firm. She had been an investigator for almost two years.

"Beth, you got nabbed last evening didn't you?" Shanice asked. "What was the rush?"

What followed was the important process of shoptalk. Like a team in the sanctity of a private locker room, the members hashed out the game they were playing. They shared the winning strategies and the losses as well. They supported each other. Even the most experienced pros learned from the rookies, but perhaps more importantly here they could laugh. Like a game of tag, the conference room was safe base. And not unlike a diver with the bends every one of them had to decompress to stay healthy and functional.

Grist for the mill included a form of black comedy. They could never share case details with others outside the group, including names, as such was held strictly confidential by law. But here they could laugh in the face of injury or even death. They could skewer senseless people they encountered, including any injurious caretaker or opposing player in the league.

Further, they could laugh at themselves. Often they described their efforts as the antics of a circus clown. Beth, with a self-deprecating sense of humor, chose this option. She told a very short version of the events of the night before, but she gave no details about the family with whom she had spent the entire evening. Rather, she brought her coworkers to giggling fits and tears, exaggerating the size of the penis as well as her own reactions to the encounter. Then she toned it down and explained the medical aspects of this rather rare occurrence and in so doing put it back into perspective and enlightened those present with still another learning experience.

Shoptalk was extremely important to all of the child abuse investigators. They were on the front line of defense for children who could not protect themselves. When they made a decision to intervene between child and parent, they had to be right. If they failed to do so, and the child was further injured or neglected, there was no question. They were wrong. The pressure from the nature of the job could be intense. All of them paid a price.

Exposure to physically abused, neglected, and abandoned kids slowly wounded the soul. Like exposure to the invisible rays of a dangerous radioactive substance, their experiences burned in their guts. All risked the growth of ugly cancerous tumors. Like veteran cops on the streets or line troops under fire, they could walk around in pain and turmoil, growing bitter and despondent with the struggle. Some social workers could and did cross the line.

Here in private they laughed directly into the very face of tragedy, utter hopelessness, and despair. Like chemotherapy,

Beth's belly busting tale and the resultant silliness in the tiny conference room helped alleviate the pain and restore the mind, body, and spirit.

Beth had just finished her story when into the room walked one William Joseph Kraznasky, otherwise known as Bill or Mr. Bill to his coworkers and friends.

"Good morning all," he said smiling.

"Back at you, Mr. Bill," the others responded in kind.

He had heard giggles from down the hall and wanted to know what he missed. So, Beth had to go all over it all one more time. The ones who had heard it before laughed all over again.

Mr. Bill, the only male investigator in the unit at that time, looked young for his age. His hands and feet were small and his face was youthful and angelic like a choirboy. Some of his colleagues teased him for never having to shave. He was short and thin in a body that seemed to belong to a teen. A shock of unruly black hair and pale grey eyes that shunned the light always made it appear like he just got out of bed. Also, he seemed to fight to avoid eye contact with people like a kid that had disobeyed his parents, or someone who was hiding a really good inside joke. But Mr. Bill was no shrinking violet. He was absolutely fearless. Like a teenage driver on the road, he gave no evidence that he recognized his own vulnerability. He drove fast and took chances. And he loved the feeling of the wind in his face as he raced through his day, his work not a chore, but a thrilling roller coaster ride.

A little girl he had saved from a beating gave him the Mr. Bill tag several years ago. She just laid it right on him, and it stuck. Bill had gone out to investigate an abuse report and simply walked in on a father in the process of thrashing his daughter with an electric cord. Hearing cries, Bill burst in the front door and managed to get the man to stop.

Mr. Bill told many versions of his intervention, including one whereby he punched the huge man out with the equivalent of a Mike Tyson left hook. But in truth Bill's entry into the living room was so spectacular that the fellow actually just stepped back in awe and confusion.

Bill ran in the house and stepped right on a stuffed bunny on a smooth linoleum floor. The bunny shot out from under his foot like a furry rocket and actually hit the far wall, knocking down a framed picture of President Kennedy, while Bill went flying backwards, like being hit by a grenade. The father was so shocked he forgot his anger in an instant and helped Bill to his feet, showing great compassion for the doofus who had so violently invaded his home.

Bill made no effort to hide the fact that he liked his nickname. He wore it proudly almost as a combat medal of sorts, a purple heart for wounds received in battle, although he had suffered little more than a bruised butt.

After all, it reminded him that he had made a difference, a real visible difference for an entire family. Many times the investigative staff yearned for even the slightest signs that their work was meaningful. They were on the front lines. They investigated, made decisions, went to court to testify, and otherwise arranged to place parents and children in contact with others child welfare staff that worked long term to resolve the family problems. Often they never knew how things worked out. They just lost track as they continued to get bombarded with more and more new abuse and neglect reports.

This case was different. The father actually faced assault charges and the child welfare agency decided to hold their abuse case in abeyance pending the outcome of the criminal matter. Actually they never did file a dependency petition. It wasn't necessary. In criminal court he drew a sentence of four weekends in jail having been given a chance to continue working. The father definitely had issues, but he was willing to address them. He became a changed man. Bill credited anger management classes, a few wonderful volunteers from a Christian jail ministry, and of course, his own masterful counseling. Since the long term, supervisory arm of the child welfare agency, protective services, was not involved, Bill dropped by to see the guy once a week for a time just to see how he was doing. To this day, the new man, his wife, and the little girl still sent Mr. Bill Christmas cards thanking him.

After finishing his coffee, Bill cornered Beth. "I want to talk to you later, Beth. Do you have some time? I think I may have a starvation case on my hands, and I want to run it by you."

"Give me about an hour; I want to clean up my office work today," replied Beth. "I still haven't completed that survey from the central office. I can't believe how they can come up with more and more busy work," she said coldly.

"I nailed that the day Cletus gave it to me," Mr. Bill said. "Make up stuff if you have to. How many of your investigations in the past year have involved families that reside in a rental property? Fifty-one! Yep, exactly Fifty-one! The question doesn't even make sense! Beth that survey will be handed over to a bunch of interns to tally and then it will find the bottom of a file drawer somewhere. You know that."

"You just made it up?" Beth asked with a grin.

"Hell no! I spent hours on that thing. That's my story and I'm sticking to it," Mr. Bill replied.

"I'll see you in an hour," Beth said, knowing full well that Mr. Bill would give her forty- five minutes, tops

The group dispersed around 7:45 and found their way to their offices. Mr. Bill already had a new neglect report waiting for him. In addition he had several collateral contacts lined up, home visits with non-family members who could help him verify his own assessment of several pending cases. Shanice had three in-office appointments scheduled in fifty-minute intervals starting at 8:00. Beth found her small office, yanked out an eight-page survey and started to answer the questions properly. When she realized that some of the answers would require pulling and reading every case file, she considered trying it Mr. Bill's way. In any case, they all got busy.

Vicky Snow was running late. Like Beth, she had been out and about last evening as well, but for different reasons. Vicky was a disheveled bleached blonde with curves everywhere, most, but not all very flattering. She tended to wear skirts that were just an inch or so too short and blouses and shirts that were just a little bit too tight. She always appeared like she hurried to get dressed. Though not really that attractive, men found her so. She was flirtatious, fun to be with and had the look of someone who could also be fun in bed. Bottom line though, she was deadly serious about her work and had a well deserved reputation for excellent instincts in the field. Some said she was particularly good at getting men to open up and speak honestly with her. And in truth, she was.

Vicky had met her current boy friend, Sal, for dinner and had allowed herself to be lured to his apartment for the night. She had run back to her place, showered, dressed for work, dashed out the door with a granola bar stuck in her mouth, and somehow careened her way to the office without killing herself. But, even so, she was still forty-five minutes late when she slipped into the building and ran smack dab into Cletus Jones who was returning to his office from a visit with his boss, Marlon Munch, Area Supervisor.

Other than a standard good morning greeting, he didn't say a thing. He just walked past Vicky and headed straight to his own office. Cletus knew well that the agency never did pay the investigators for the actual time they worked. In truth they were instructed to claim comp-time for anything over 80 hours in the two-week payroll time period. Actually finding time to use comp was the problem. It just piled up on the books. Most worked hundreds of work hours in a given year for which they never would be compensated.

Cletus' home away from home was located adjacent to a large fully equipped clerical station. This bay was the hub of the operation, central to other offices used by the investigative staff. There he found his secretary busy with a stack of file jackets. He walked right past him without so much as a Hello and slumped into his oversized swivel chair.

Trouble, Ernie thought. And without delay he followed his boss into his office.

"Good morning," Mr. Jones. "Is there anything I can do for you?"

"No, I'm just fine," said the boss with enough sarcasm to clearly show he wasn't.

"Are you sure?" prodded Ernie.

"You read me like a book, don't you? I met with Munch this morning. I won't be filling the vacant position. Please don't tell the staff anything yet, but I think we are getting someone assigned to us from another unit somewhere outside of our district. A hundred to one it's going to be some jerk from Miami. I can just sense it. Damn, you watch, we are getting set up for a loser that they didn't have the balls to fire."

"I'm sorry Ernie. I shouldn't talk like that. It's just that we never seem to catch a break."

"Maybe it won't be quite that bad. As my mother used to say, don't borrow trouble before it comes," Ernie said cheerfully.

"I know, but the troops have been pushing a heavy sled long enough. Up hill, too! That includes you Ernie. We have had the Clerk Typist position frozen for almost two years! You are carrying the work of two people and no one gives a damn. They give us positions and then freeze them to save money, or order us to fill them with the bastard son of a congressman! Cripes!"

"Sleds? What are you talking about?" Ernie asked.

"Never mind."

"Oh. One more thing," Cletus tossed out just as Ernie turned to leave. "Did I give El the whole week off?" Cletus asked referring to the last of his investigators.

"Yes, you did. She is sick, remember."

"We are getting so many reports coming in it's not funny. I have got to get this vacancy filled or the troops are all going to be sick," moaned Cletus.

"We will be fine, Mr. Jones. You have a good staff, and they will rest when things slow down."

"Ernie," Cletus said with half a smile.

"Please call me Cletus."

Chapter 3

Mr. Bill appeared suddenly in Beth's office. She glanced at her watch. He had given her a half hour tops.

"What's on your mind, Mr. Bill?" she asked.

"I have been working on a case that came in almost two months ago. The reporter, a teacher, was worried that a little girl, age six, was not being fed properly. Sure enough the girl, Bernice, was very thin. I interviewed everyone that I could. Then I had her checked by the medical review team. I just received their report. They concluded that she was under weight for her age, below 5% on the BMI, so that is a red flag right there. But, they could not conclude that she was undernourished or ill fed. Her mother, Clarissa James, age thirty-nine, is a Black, unmarried woman employed at the technical college as a secretary. She has several college level credits under her belt and hopes to get a degree in psychology and eventually work as a student advisor. She presented very well. She explained that her child had been ill for a while. There seemed to be nothing to it."

"The mother's living situation bothered me a little. She owns a small rundown bungalow but lives with another woman. This gal said she was forty-nine but looked older. She is not related to the mother and does not appear to be a friend or anything like that. She was introduced as a roommate, one Maria Marcelin. As far as I can tell, this woman doesn't contribute anything to the household although she supposedly is a fortuneteller. There is a hand made sign hanging out front. She is not employed and can't possibly bring in any money with that. She just seems to live there."

"Also, this old gal gave off some strange vibes when I talked to her. It was nothing I could put my finger on. Absolutely nothing. This is going to sound like BS, but I didn't like her eyes. She has fish eyes that look like they may pop out of the sockets at any time. Believe me those eyes gave me the willies. She had a way of staring at me even when I was not looking at her. I could feel some intensity in that stare. When I did make direct eye contact with her, she seemed to be looking right through me, or something. Anyway, I haven't closed it because it just doesn't feel right. Cletus wants me to fish or cut bait. Now! The case is flagged on the computer as overdue for disposition."

"I remember you talking some about this case before. I thought that you had closed it out long ago," Beth said.

"I'll get to the point. I called the reporter day before yesterday, and she is still very concerned. There is nothing much there, but she still feels like something is wrong. She said the little girl is just too quiet. Bottom line, Beth, I want you to go out there with me today and get your own reading."

"Gee! Bill," Beth sighed. " I'm behind on some things and...."

"I'll finish that survey for you, if you want," Mr. Bill interjected. "I need help with this one, Beth."

Beth paused. She knew before he barged into her office that she would help him. The investigators often hashed out things with each other; it helped confirm their own opinions, or, in some cases, put them on a totally different track. But there was really no question in this kind of case. She would not necessarily be doing Mr. Bill a favor. She would be fulfilling an extremely important role in helping the lead investigator come to a conclusion. In this case, it could literally mean life or death.

"Deal," she said, pushing the damnable survey across the desk toward him. "I'll come get you around 3:00," he replied.

After he left, Beth rummaged in her desk for an article she had saved on starvation cases. She reread it concluding that there was nothing much to help them there. Then she got back to her files and the computer. She grabbed a yogurt from the snack bar in the adjoining juvenile court complex for lunch and ate it at her desk, still plugging away.

Bill barged into her office at 3:30 P.M. sharp and tossed her completed survey on her desk. Beth had been so lost in her work she had completely forgotten about him and wondered for a split second why he was there. When she recovered, she jumped up and prepared to go. An escape from the office, the phone calls, and the computer was welcomed.

Mr. Bill and Beth Jacoby discussed how they would approach the caregivers as he drove them out to work the James case. They agreed to try a strategy used sometimes by the police. First, they both would enter the house with antennas up trying to pick up on any signals that might help them decide what if anything was amiss in the home. Then one would ask questions while the other studied the two women for reactions, nervousness or any other physical cues that might indicate lying or deceit.

Clarissa James lived in a modest cottage made of brick with contractor grade windows and trim. There was an older

Ford Focus parked on a small concrete pad made to get a single vehicle off the street. Steppingstones led to a simple slab at the front door that was covered by an overhang that might have provided shelter for one person to fish for keys from a pocket or purse in the rain. They rang the bell and waited.

Clarissa had been expecting Bill Kraznasky, but it was obvious she was somewhat surprised to see someone with him. But when Bill made introductions, they were cordially invited in. Beth checked out the mother carefully. She was attractive, polite, well spoken, and accommodating. Beth jumped to the assumption that she and Bill would quickly resolve any questions about this household one way or the other.

Unfortunately, they left within a short time, both extremely frustrated. In truth they learned nothing more about the family. The little girl was somewhat withdrawn and thin, but not overly so. The mother seemed relaxed and appropriate. But, Maria Marcelin, the other adult in the home, had not been there. When he learned this, Bill became angry. He pressed the mother hard about the roommate's absence and was not satisfied with her plea that she did not know that Maria's presence was required. Unfortunately Bill knew it was his fault. He had just assumed that the so-called roommate would be there and had not made the point that she be present.

He was really steamed, but he had no one to blame but himself. He calmed down long enough to tell Clarissa James that he would be back tomorrow, and he fully expected Maria Marcelin to be there.

Actually the visit was not a total waste of time. Beth spotted a hint of unwarranted anxiety in the mother's response to Bill's frustration. Clarissa seemed to be worried but not necessarily about them. Having missed the real target of their investigation and wasting time, the investigators did not linger. They excused themselves and hurried off. Bill let out a stream of curses as he yanked his car from the curb and sped away like a thief from the scene of a crime.

They got back to their building a little after four. Bill charged past Ernie at his desk with out saying a word, Beth tailing several yards behind. Bill barged into his office and slammed his leather bound notebook across his desk. The case slid straight into a pile of computer paper and sent it all flying before taking out a half full coffee cup with a deafening crash.

"What happened?" Ernie cried, shaken by Bill's show of anger.

"Let him be, Ernie," responded Beth. "He's mad at himself for not ensuring that Mrs. James' roommate would be home for our visit. I tried to calm him down, but he was having none of that. He'll be fine after a while. I guess we will have to do another visit to find out what this older woman is like and what is really going on out there."

Ernie busied himself with his work, but he had been shaken by Mr. Bill's frustration. The staff was his family, and he hated the fact that they bore so many burdens.

He knew that the agency itself was the source of most of them. The central office in Tallahassee bombarded the Area Supervisor's office with a steady stream of demands that seemed to have little to do with constructive time with parents and children. Much of that burden fell directly on the line staff. New laws. New rules. New policies. New procedures. All of it a tinkering process generated by the agency in response to powerful forces inside and outside of the agency that never seemed to end.

Ernie and the others understood that the entire child welfare agency was absolutely vulnerable to a child's death or serious injury particularly if there was evidence that all laws, rules, policies, and procedures were not followed. One of the worse case scenarios involved the investigative arm of the organization. A worker like Bill who investigates a report of abuse or neglect has two dispositions, founded or unfounded. If he concludes that the report is founded he essentially has two choices. If he has legal justification, he can remove the child temporarily. He must then set up a shelter hearing before a judge within twenty-four hours and secure approval from the bench to hold the child until further disposition of the case. The second option is to leave the child at home with cooperative parents who readily accept voluntary services or with mandatory services ordered by the court. If he concludes there is nothing to the report, he signs it off as an unfounded allegation and moves on to the next case.

Whatever his findings and subsequent action, he must be right. Removing a child from the parents is never to be taken lightly. The concept runs counter to some of the most respected tenets in society, including privacy, individual freedom, religious freedom, and most importantly, parental rights. Those investigators who prove to be heavy handed do not last long with the agency.

On the other hand, if an investigator allows the child to remain at home and the parent or caregiver murders the child or fails to protect a child from sexual assault or serious injury, there is no end to the repercussions. These are an absolute certainty whether there was a hint of danger or not. One headline case anywhere in the state always prompted swift attention from the political arena, as representatives who scrambled to seize the high moral ground attacked and condemned the agency, often without even bothering to check the facts. Thus the child welfare system seemed to remain in a constant state of flux. The entire organization seemed to crack and buckle like ice on a pond from the pressure of ever changing winds and temperatures.

Ernie had long since come to realize that the whims of politicians, high-level managers, and consultants called the shots. His very work place actually seemed to reverberate at times with noise, the proverbial noise in the system. He heard it often, a grating sound like fingernails on a chalkboard. Ernie tried very hard to silence it. The massive computer system, designed to track almost everything imaginable in an investigation was the key. It demanded data and timely input on every case. Each field in the electronic file had to be filled in and completed within specified time frames. If not, the supervisor's computer danced with a steady stream of error messages. More noise.

So, he lingered in the evenings. Although case information was to be put in the system by the investigators, he pitched in and helped by up loading completed cases. As he worked, he pondered the setback for Mr. Bill. He felt the frustration just as Bill had. He also felt the anger. He wondered if there was more he could do. He pulled up the case file on his computer and read it. The overdue completion of the James investigation screamed out at him like a banshee wailing outside in the night. More noise.

Alone with his thoughts, he pondered. He was so non aggressive and he knew it, but, every day more reports concerning abused or neglected children poured in. He wished that he were capable of striking back somehow, stopping the flow.

Ernie had a dark place into which he would retreat once in awhile. It materialized as a child as he experienced taunts from bullies. In his dark place, he was strong and fearless. He fought back! So now, alone in the office, he let himself go there. Anger grew and dark images of violent child abusers emerged. He lashed out at them and made them hurt. Made them stop.

Chapter 4

She had waited. She had waited for the whore.

There had been some heavy drinking going on for several hours. She had watched her leave the bar giggling and stumbling, able to stand upright only with the support of the man with her. They had piled into a rusty blue Impala and slowly eased out into the street. She had slumped down a little as they drove past. Then she started up her own car and followed, waiting awhile before pulling on her headlights. She kept an eye on the Impala as it crept in and out of the circles of light under the street lamps. She had not been afraid of losing them. She knew where they were going anyway.

She had pulled over almost a full block from the house and watched as the man parked and helped the woman out of the car. Even at that distance she had heard the woman laughing with a voice much too loud for the hour. They had entered. A few minutes had elapsed, and a young boy had emerged. The boy lit a cigarette, walked down the street toward the spot where she was parked, but quickly turned and vanished up an alley. She quickly figured out who the boy was and thought no more about him.

Now, she fidgeted with her hair net and double-checked for her hospital mask, gown, gloves, slippers, and flashlight. Then she waited some more.

The man took about a half an hour to finish his business. Then he too left the house and climbed into his car. In a minute he was gone. Just to make sure, she waited, giving the drunken woman time to pass out on her bed. Then she quietly opened the driver's door, slipped out, and made her way up the street. She paused at the back of the house in the shadows and donned her protective gear. Next she found the open window in the back. The screen was no problem as it popped right out in her hands, just as she had practiced it.

She slid into a sewing room of sorts, but in the process she managed to kick over an old TV tray and a box of buttons. The room was littered and piled high with material, ends, pieces, and the like. While the tray did make some noise, it was partially muffled by a soft landing. The intruder was not worried in the least. She could hear pig-like grunts and snorts from the bedroom.

As she slipped down the hall, her light flashed on dirty tissues, broken toys and just plain crap on the floor, the debris and waste of a sordid lifestyle that the whore never seemed to notice. The place smelled of stale cigarettes, beer, and filth. The cockroaches slithering through the mess gave her the creeps, so she moved on with real purpose.

She found the woman nude, sprawled out on her bed, her fat legs partially covered with the top sheet. She immediately pulled out a large, butcher knife, grabbed the woman by the hair, arched back her head, and slit her throat. The knife cut very deep. The only sound the victim could manage was a hideous gasping of sorts as life spilled out of her and spread like a black shadow across the bed.

She placed the knife in a large Zip-Lock bag, pulled off the bloody gloves, dropped them in as well, and took the time to put on another pair. Later she would discard all the necessary paraphernalia of the kill.

The nine-month old baby was in her crib.

She roused the child and whispered to her in soft soothing tones. The little girl hardly stirred, allowing herself to be picked up and carried away without so much as a whimper.

Typical, the woman thought. The poor kid probably had been tossed around to any and all from the time she was born. She would have known lots of strangers. So too, she knew no strangers at all. Her mother was too occupied by her own problems. But they were not an issue now. Mama would no longer haunt the bars seeking ready cash for transactions in the alley. Nor would she find simple comfort in the arms of anyone who would compliment her and drive her home.

She gently eased the child into the car seat then motored around a little to help the baby fall back to sleep. Then she drove to his house, parking a good way off. After donning a fresh pair of gloves, she walked to where his Impala was parked on the street. She quietly inspected the trunk and found it wired shut with a rusty coat hanger. She knew about the punched out trunk lock and the coat hanger too.

With a fresh pair of gloves on, she untwisted the wire and opened the trunk. Inside, she carefully hid the knife behind a loose spare tire, and for good measure, tossed some old rags she found in the trunk over and around the hiding place. After carefully refastening the coat hanger, she returned to her car and drove away into the night.

Chapter 5

Shanice Gooding burst into the building a few minutes before 7:00 A.M. She had been up since 3:15 A.M. and it showed. Her hair was a mess and her outfit disheveled. She looked like a used Barbie that had been the favorite of a four year old who never could get the tiny clothes back on right. If she had been thinking about how she looked, she would have been appalled.

"Is Cletus in yet?" she called out to no one in particular as she burst into the conference room. It was empty. Even Ernie had not made it in yet. She turned, found her office, and slumped into a chair. She was still wound tight as a drum, her nerves unsettled like a thoroughbred that had just run the Belmont Stakes in the mud.

She had been on call and roused in the middle of the night by one of the worst kind of reports, domestic violence. Even most cops hated them. Tension was always elevated when an officer knocked on the door, not really knowing what the reception might be. You could walk right into what appeared to be a simple marital spat and end up with a terrible knife wound on your face or a bullet in the gut.

This one was a mess. Both parents were drunk, and the pair was obviously going at it. The first cop on the scene called for backup before he even got out of the car, so furious the angry voices blasting through the thin walls of the double-wide. He had walked to the front door and paused for a few minutes, giving his backup some time to arrive, and simply listened to the clash of one man and one woman who probably once thought they would grow old together in marital bliss. Both were landing blows.

It was then that he heard a child. Or was it two. Yes, it had sounded like two voices screaming out in real horror, combining into a plea so desperate that the officer had not hesitated any longer. He speed dialed dispatch to send for child welfare immediately, then turned and smashed the door into a pile of broken glass and particle board and flew into the living room.

The brave cop had held the two at bay until reinforcements had arrived. Then two more police officers barged into the trailer and collectively, they did their thing. They tased the wild-eyed White male who had cussed and spit in a literal pink froth of demented anger, roughly cuffing his butt and tossing him on the floor. His face was a bloody mask but not from anything they had done. His wife had clobbered her beloved with a frying pan, still partially full of grease. A rather large split had opened across his forehead, and it steadily seeped blood down his face. Large gobs of spittle and gore flew from his lips as he squealed like a wounded, trussed up, greased pig waiting to be slaughtered.

They had seen the type many times. Mr. Leonard Samford, as they would learn later, was a piece of work. He looked every bit like the thug he was. He had a huge head that fronted an ugly face made up with features badly out of symmetry with each other. The beady black eyes were too small and close together. The fleshy mouth was too large. On top of that, his upper lip was curled in a perpetual, I don't give a shit, sneer.

He was probably 30 but looked much older, his dirty black hair already showing some grey. He wore it pulled back in a ridiculously small pony tail that stuck straight out from the back of his head, like cartoon depictions of Popeye's girl friend Olive Oyl. He sported numerous cheap tattoos including four letter words on the back of each hand, spelled out one letter at a time just below the knuckles. In addition numerous rudely drawn symbols, including a cross and a swastika, adorned his neck. Some muscle tone remained on his arms but a growing inner tube around his waist spoke of two much beer, too many French fries, and a whole world of hate

But Daddy was not the victim here. It was obvious that he had been beating his wife for some time. That would include years. This time it was an unknown interval stretching from the start of the battle right up to the moment the good guys arrived.

Mom looked like she had gone ten rounds with Muhammad Ali, her face swollen and lumpy, both eyes closing rapidly with open cuts below the brows and ugly contusions on her arms, left cheek, and ear. She looked like she had been down this road before. Very thin and haggard, like Twiggy on methamphetamines, she could have passed for fifty. With her face scarred and marred, she no longer could even pretend that she was once an attractive girl. Neither had actually fought the police perhaps because they had been staring down a gun barrel from the moment the first responder walked right through the door, but they had clobbered each other with effect.

Both were told that they were going to jail. Domestic violence. And they had no real problem with that no doubt because they had been there before. But they missed the point that an investigator from child welfare would be there to take care of their children.

That had all changed when Shanice walked in. It was then that they realized that their dear babies were going to be ripped from their collective bosom. Now they had a target who was not armed and dangerous, a common enemy, a victim for all the venom still raging in their veins. And, for Christ sake, she was Black!

"No fucking Nigger is going to lay hands on my babies!" mother had shouted before Shanice had said a word, her voice bristling with a full measure of righteous indignation.

Then the parents cranked up the volume all over again. Both combatants went right back into the wildly agitated state in which they had been found. Little mother had to be wrestled down and cuffed as well. They loosed a steady stream of almost unintelligible curses at the new arrival and writhed on the floor like possessed by demons. It was all the cops could do to control themselves. The officer who had torn off the door to get in was a split-second away from losing it and stomping both of them into silence. He literally had to excuse himself for a moment to walk back outside to breathe.

Shanice froze. She stood speechless and inert. She had been the target of terrific anger before, but this was different. All her life she had been somewhat sheltered by her parents. She had attended private elementary and secondary schools and a fine Ivy League institution. Association with others who shared her family's means and values had framed her social life. She had never experienced anything so vile in her life, and she was shaken to the core. Her body began to react to the abuse. Her muscles tightened and acid flowed in her gut. She began to gently sway and her legs began to fail her. She might have stood there transfixed until she fell from nervous exhaustion had not one of the cops grabbed her by the arm and led her out of the room. He managed to seize her attention by reminding her that there were children in the house that needed her help.

Shanice found two little girls, probably three and four, hiding in a bedroom closet. Both of them had been terrorized by the violence they had witnessed. They had simply wanted to escape the noise, the spine twisting screams of their parents at war. The combatants had relaxed just a bit when the police arrived and now, it had all started up again. Shanice nearly cried as she hugged them close to her breast trying to protect them to smother out the clamor that so desperately frightened them.

Finally, she entered the living room with the children each hugging a leg like their lives depended on it. She had to try to speak to the parents although all she really wanted to do was flee with her charges and find them a place of refuge out of the storm. But even though they were cuffed up like madmen in straight jackets, their mouths worked just fine. Shanice learned that she was an ignorant pick-ninny, a two-bit whore, and a filthy bitch.

Daddy stayed clear of directly threatening her, but he promised to have another visit with her soon. When one of the cops warned him to shut up or get additional charges, he closed his ugly, pie hole, but only until he could think of something else to say.

"Who the hell is your supervisor?" he had snarled, being as polite as he could possibly be.

"Mr. Cletus Jones," Shanice replied beginning to find herself again. "You can locate both of us in the children's services building down town."

"Oh, another blessed Nigger. Cletus! That figures. You tell that boy I'll be in his stinking office as soon as I bail out. And, you make sure he damn well understands I want my kids back right then and there. You got that Sugar?" he had added.

The cops had been impatient to get out of there. They loaded up their passengers and delivered them straight to jail. Shanice lingered to get some clothes and toys for the little ones. Then she spent a long time soothing and reassuring them. Finally she found car seats in her trunk, strapped them in, and drove them to a shelter home. She introduced the children to the trained shelter parents and sat with them until they seemed comfortable there. She put them to bed and kissed both of them gently as they slipped quietly into a restful sleep. Then she drank some tea with the shelter parents and went over all the information that she had on the children which wasn't much more than their names. Finally after two hours, she excused herself and left, actually stumbling light-headedly, as she walked out the front door. Even though stars still flickered above in an inky sky, it would be light in an hour or so.

Chapter 6

Dave Boyette, city cop, Atmore, Alabama, had been parked out near Interstate 65, looking to nab a late night speeder or a DUI that might happen to pass. At 4:30 A.M. he was fighting a strong urge to just nod off for a few minutes when his radio squawked him awake. He listened to the message intently, his tired eyes moving rapidly from a lazy squint to wide-open, like he had just seen a ghost. But it was what he had been hearing that grabbed his full attention. He clicked his seat belt, cranked up the engine, and flew back toward town, sirens wailing. The blue lights flickered and flashed on the telephone poles as he sped by, like each had somehow attracted the attention of the paparazzi.

He careened into the parking lot of the Bethel AME Church, hopped out and immediately went to the entryway, a covered porch of sorts where the congregation often mingled before and after services. To the right side of the doors, right where dispatch had said it would be, was a cardboard carton, the top loosely closed. He carefully opened the flaps. Inside, wrapped in what appeared to be a pink blanket, was a baby. It was breathing softly with not a care in the world, fast asleep. Dave stood over it for a minute. Maybe it was the setting. After all, he was at a church. He could not help but make a connection between this child and another baby that had also slept in a humble, makeshift crib.

The cop walked away for a moment, opened the trunk of his car and pulled on a pair of gloves. A glance reaffirmed that he was not carrying an infant's car seat. He smiled at the fact that he would now break a few laws transporting the kid. He returned to the church and carefully carried baby, box, and all back to the car. He placed the carton on the passenger seat wedging it in between the back of the seat and the dashboard. That would have to do, he thought.

Dave drove carefully, like he was hauling a cargo of loose eggs, straight to the town's small emergency facility, radioing in advance for the child welfare people. There was no physician on duty but the night nurse agreed to give the child a thorough health examination. Dave, conscious of collecting whatever evidence he could, first asked the nurse to glove up and help him retrieve the child from the box. She lifted the baby from under the arms while he unwound the blanket. The nurse announced that the child was a girl, and they exchanged a smile. There was nothing else at all in the box, so Dave secured the two items and set them aside for later examination by a crime scene technician.

Chapter 7

Later that morning Shanice jumped Cletus the moment he walked in. He winked at Ernie to excuse them and closed the door behind her. He recognized immediately that she had had a bad experience, the kind that tears you up inside. Thankfully they were relatively rare, even though the investigators normally walked into fire several times over the course of a year. Cletus knew that Shanice had confronted something very different. She was normally tough as nails but this time she was shaken. They ended up talking for almost an hour.

"I somehow thought that racism like that was disappearing," she said.

"Not yet. But things have improved, Shanice," he offered.

"You have handled jerks like that before haven't you?"

"Yes, but these people were right out front with their hatred. And, they went from trying to kill one another to attacking me in less than a minute, just because I am a Black woman. The mother was just as vicious as the father. Frankly Cletus they scared me. They might as well have had burning torches and hoods. And please understand that that bastard is coming over here to see you as soon as he can. Maybe you should get a guard or something. He may bring a gun."

"Whoa! Hold on," Cletus replied.

"Don't forget, they are reacting like almost any parent who loses their kids to us. Think about how hard that hurts. He will come in here going crazy, and I honestly think I would too. The racist stuff is just a cover that makes it a little more difficult to handle. I can deal with him, Shanice."

"Well great then," she snapped sarcastically. "I hope that goes well for you. Excuse me for taking up so much of your time." She turned toward the door but did not leave the room.

Cletus dropped his eyes. He knew he had screwed up. He had not heard her out. She was bleeding internally, and he had cheerfully slapped a Spiderman band-aid on her little finger like she was a child with a paper cut.

"I'm sorry, Shanice. I wasn't listening. I jumped into my damn know-it-all mode. I sure as hell didn't mean to make it sound like it was nothing," Cletus said softly.

She turned back and looked at him. A few tears fell from her eyes, but she stifled them quickly.

"Just let me talk a little," she said.

And he did. And he listened well. Later, Shanice summed up how she felt.

"I was a very good student as you know. You have seen my academic achievement records. I guess I am as well informed as anyone I know about Black History. Intellectually I can match you or anyone else on the subject of racism. But, Cletus, I guess I really didn't know anything about it at all. I didn't know how it felt until last night."

"To tell you the truth, Cletus, I wish I had never gone through that. Today, the world seems darker, and I'm afraid the sun will never fully shine again. I'm not sure I want to spend any more time here either. I have been cursed before. I have been hurt before. That's part of this job. But I will not bathe myself in human misery until my world is colored by it. I don't have to. I am going to stay with it for a while. But understand me. If I can't shake the feeling that my heart and soul will not survive unscathed, I'm out of here. I will gladly leave these people to you, and you can deal with them, as you say."

"Look, I hear you, and I understand. I am so sorry you had to go through that. I talk tough but I never experienced anything but a few taunts and stuff. I have no idea what I would have done last night if it had been me. Your feelings are real. Take some time to think about it. Take some time off if you want. But, I do want you to know something as you think it over. You are very good at this kind of work. You are a gift to these kids and their parents, and you are absolutely in the right calling as far as I am concerned. I don't want you to leave. And that's not just because I will have another vacancy. I don't want you to leave because you are the very type of person that these kids and their parents need to know. You bring much more to the job than you realize."

"Thanks, Cletus," Shanice said as she rose to go.

"Seriously, watch out for this guy. He can get under your skin; I promise you."

"I'll be careful with him," Cletus said.

And then rather uncharacteristically for the big man, he got up, took her hand, and smiled at her. She smiled back, thanked him again, and walked out the door.

Chapter 8

Mr. Bill and Beth Jacoby took their lunch hour and drove back to the home of Clarissa James. This time Maria Marcelin was there. But, both Bill and Beth immediately noticed defiance in her eyes. She was definitely not pleased to see them. In addition, Clarissa was on edge. They went through some preliminaries and then turned their focus on the older woman. They both peppered her with questions. They pressed hard on how she came to live there. They wanted to know about her financial contributions to the household. They asked about her relationship with the child, Bernice.

She was managing fine until Mr. Bill asked her if she enjoyed babysitting for Clarissa.

"I don't like being alone with her," Maria said.

"Is she a disciplinary problem?" he asked.

"No!" she snapped. "Not at all."

"She does as I say!"

Beth was watching Maria intently. The force of her answer was very unusual. It was as if she had let down her guard for a second and hinted at something that troubled her.

"Well. Why would you be reluctant to be alone with Bernice?" Bill asked incredulously.

The woman took too long before she attempted an answer. Both Beth and Bill noticed the pregnant pause. Maria seemed to be agitated. Beth took her eyes off her long enough to get a glimpse of Clarissa. She was nervous too, a look of dread in her expression and a few beads of perspiration on her upper lip. But it was not because of the tension of the interview. There was real fear written on her face.

Maria recovered quickly and told Bill she did not like the responsibility of caring for a child. She went on to say with a slight smile that she was getting too old to run after the little ones.

After that, Maria was amicable and pleasant. The pair of investigators left gaining little else of importance.

In the car on the way back to the office, however, they could not be still. They had learned something after all. Maria seemed to fear Bernice, a willowy, shy little girl. What was that, they kept asking each other.

"You know." Bill said, "her response about not wanting to be responsible for a little one would have made absolute sense. But, she had just told us in no uncertain terms that Bernice did as she was told! Why would one be afraid of a child, particularly an obedient child?"

"I'm not sure but Maria wasn't the only one displaying fear in that house," Beth answered. "Clarissa was almost shaking when you were pushing Maria. There is something weird going on there," offered Beth.

They both fell silent for a time as Bill weaved his way through traffic. After cussing at a slow vehicle driven by a white haired old man that made him miss a light, Bill brought the car to a halt. In the sixty seconds the light took to change, Bill had a revelation.

"Hey, this will sound crazy, but what if they are both afraid of Bernice because she is more than a just a child," Bill said excitedly.

"What do you mean?" Beth followed without understanding.

"What if she is haunted or something!" Bill shot back.

"Do you mean possessed?"

"Yea, possessed!" Bill crowed, with a big smile on his face. "Maria is a fortuneteller, right? And she was raised in the West Indies. She probably believes in that stuff. Maybe she got to Clarissa too."

"As wild as it sounds, it does make sense," offered Beth. "Maybe limiting the child's food has something to do with controlling evil spirits," she added.

We need to get the psych boys in on this," Bill went on. "They can evaluate all three of them through the medical review team. Simple, right?"

"I want to watch you explain that to Cletus," Beth said smiling. If you can get him to buy that he will clear the computer for another time extension and you are home free," Beth offered.

"Thanks, Beth. I really needed some help. I knew there was something there and you helped me confirm it. I owe you one, even though I did put in several hours with that survey," he said with a wink.

"Oh, hours and hours," Beth concluded. "Right."

Chapter 9

The day went by quickly, and Cletus forgot about the father of the year in the midst of the normal routine. As he reviewed cases on his computer late in the afternoon, he sensed someone behind him. He swiveled around in his chair and found a classic looking bad ass jerk looming in his doorway.

"You Cletus?" the man snapped, like the words themselves had to be spit out rather than said.

Cletus recognized him immediately. Leonard Samford. His forehead was bound with a large swath of muslin. He looked a little like the fife player in the Spirit Of 76 icon, a man with shoulder length black hair accented by the white bandage. Of course that piper didn't sport Nazi tattoos. Leonard's shirt still bore signs of grease and blood. The ponytail was gone. The officers at the jail would have taken the filthy piece of cloth that had secured it. Gee, he might have hung himself with it, Cletus mourned.

"Yes, I'm Mr. Jones," Cletus replied flatly, "how can I help you?"

"I've come for my children, and I want them now!" the man demanded.

"You must be Leonard Samford?" Cletus offered.

"That's right, and I want my children back now."

Cletus thought about making the man get an appointment. After all, he seldom if ever just dropped what he was doing for people walking right in his office while he was working. He decided he might as well get it over with.

"The judge placed your children in shelter care at a hearing this morning," Cletus began.

"I don't think you are listening to me. I was in the fucking jail this morning and could not be there for no hearing. Those are my children, and I want them back. Make sure you understand. I'm not leaving here without them. You got that, Boy?"

Cletus smiled and took a moment. The scene playing out before him reminded him of the time he had called out a senior on the football team in high school. Cletus had made demands too although he had long since forgotten what the contention was. The linebacker had ended the confrontation by kicking his butt, hard and decisively in front of most of the team. Cletus had learned a lot right then and there about provocative language, and threats. One better be able to back them up.

"Mr. Samford," Cletus began, trying to offset the obvious slur with the formal address. "I understand that you are upset. We did in fact remove your children from your custody and place them in shelter care. We asked the judge for a court order to hold them, and we got it. You are not getting your children back until you convince the judge that..."

"Fuck you! You have no power over me. You are nothing but a stinking low life Nigger! Get your boss in here. Now!"

"No! I won't do that. I'm the one you have to deal with. I make the decisions here. Understand?"

Leonard Samford's face turned beet red. Violence lurked in his body language and loomed in his eyes. He closed the distance between them to less than a yard and balled up his fists.

"I'll ask one more time," Leonard almost whispered. Then raising his voice a little and accenting each word, he snarled even more than usual with that curl in his upper lip, "Get your boss in here or I am going to wipe your fat ass all over your fucking office, right here, right now."

Cletus paused and stared directly at the man who was threatening him. He was not afraid but he was not really certain he could take down this guy either. Samford was younger and brimming with rage. Fighting him there in the crowded office would be a challenge. But, Cletus reasoned, I have been there before, and I won't back down now.

So he slowly rose out of his chair. In so doing, Leonard Samford was taken from a position where upon he looked down on his adversary to one where he had to look up. It stopped him for a second. But, the demons that raged within him would not be stilled.

From childhood Leonard had learned from an abusive, alcoholic father that Black people were the root of all that was evil. He, like Hitler blaming Jews for Germany's misery after the country's defeat in W. W. I., preached pure hatred for anyone different, anyone of color for his defeat as a man. In so doing he masked his own many deficiencies, including genes that carried very little in the way of intelligence. Now, thoroughly trained like a good storm trooper, Leonard goose-stepped on to the constant beat of his father's drum that still pounded away loudly in his head.

"I ain't afraid of you. There aren't six other Niggers standing around to jump me from behind. Go ahead, Boy, take your best shot. I'll bust your face in for you in a heart beat."

"I understand why you are upset," said Cletus with a calmness that belied the tension creeping up his neck.

"I strongly suggest that you go home and cool down. Then I will help you do the things necessary to get your children returned to you."

"You don't know who you are talking to Boy. You are just a lump of black tar in my road. I'll run over you and think nothing of it. So before you open those big purple lips you better think and do as I say else I start smashing in your face. And know this, I can easily hurt you permanent. Stomping on your black ass is like stepping on a filthy cockroach!" Samford snarled with more than a hint of violence in his voice.

Unbeknownst to the two squared off in the office, a Sheriff's Deputy moved silently into the room.

"Cletus, is there a problem here?" the deputy asked calmly, his hand clutching a slapjack that he had pulled from his belt.

"I don't have a problem but Mr. Samford here is very upset about the fact that his children must remain in shelter care for awhile. I've asked him to go home and cool down. I believe he was on the way out. Weren't you, Mr Samford?" Cletus asked coolly.

For what seemed to be an overly long time, none of the three men moved. Then Leonard Samford turned very slowly coughing as he did. Then he spit. A large ball of phlegm and spittle hit the floor right next to Cletus' shoe.

The big man jumped back in shock and surprise. That nasty sign of total disrespect jarred him almost as much as a hard slap to the face."

"Oh, I'm sorry about that," Leonard grinned sarcastically, knowing he had hit home. "Got a cold, you know," Samford added, as sarcastically as he could muster.

"Thanks for all your help, Cleat," he went on, a few drops of spit still clinging to his curled lips. Then he walked dipping his shoulders in exaggerated defiance past the deputy and out the door. Instead of just leaving he stopped in the hall, turned his head, and looked directly into Cletus' eyes.

Then he said, "I'll be seeing you around, Boy. You should try to keep me in mind because I think we have some unfinished business, don't we?"

The cop wheeled to go after the man, but Cletus caught hold of his arm.

"Don't bother with that idiot, Frank. Let him go. For the life of me I can't understand why a guy like him gets bail. According to Shanice he was wild last night, and it took three armed good guys to subdue him. I do want to thank you for coming by. I was fixing to tangle with him, and I might have wrinkled my clothes," Cletus said with false bravado.

"Hey, aren't you on duty in the court room? How did you know that I was facing some trouble?" Cletus asked.

"Ernie caught up with me," Frank said. "Thank God I didn't have court duty today. Ernie would have run into the courtroom and told the judge the building was on fire or something. I was monitoring the witness rooms when he collared me. Man, was he about to lay an egg. Then Beth and some others from down here showed up. You know, Cletus, your crew has your back. You ought to be proud of that."

"I am," said Cletus with a broad smile.

"I am."

Cletus hung around the office after 5:00. His family would be expecting him soon at home for supper. But, he was troubled. Everyone thought he was as strong as an ox and as brave as a Congressional Medal Of Honor winner. But deep inside he knew he was not. Yes, he had been a very good football player in top physical condition in the day. Even now he could count on his size alone for effect. But the years had passed. He had been riding a desk for a long time and the once formidable abs were now soft and hidden by a large spare tire.

Cletus knew that Leonard Samford had shaken him. He remembered his conversation with Shanice about her reaction to him. Now he was worried and ashamed. The crazed racist had made him feel vulnerable for the first time in his life. Cletus knew he would eventually summons the courage to walk to his car, but he could not stop thinking about the possibility that Leonard might be waiting for him in the parking lot with a baseball bat or a machete.

Cletus rifled through a lump of name cards and small slips of paper he carried in his wallet. Eventually he found the telephone number of an old friend, a teammate from Auburn he met years ago. Willis had fallen on hard times and pulled a ten-year prison sentence for aggravated assault after dropping out of school because of academic problems. Cletus had remained a loyal friend. He visited with him often, sent him cigarettes, and stayed in touch.

He and Willis still talked. Each time they did since he was released, Willis thanked him for standing by him and told him to call if Cletus ever needed help. He usually added with a laugh that he learned many skills in prison. Then he would change the tenor of his voice and say without a hint of humor that if Cletus ever needed someone who was really good at hurting people, he was available.

Cletus took out his cell phone and dialed the number. It rang about ten times. Then he hung up and cautiously walked out of the building and through the parking lot to his car, looking over his shoulder. He would try again later.

Chapter 10

The next morning Ernie made the coffee in the conference room as usual and greeted the crew as they drifted in. Vicky Snow was uncharacteristically the very first investigator to arrive.

"Morning honey," said Ernie with a smile.

"No date last night?" he teased.

"Oh come on, Ernie. I do more than date. I have a life you know," she responded.

"Have you taken up growing orchids or something?" Ernie joked.

"Hey, bite me Ernie!" she snapped, resurrecting an old comeback used by the boys she knew well in high school.

"Morning!" offered Beth as she charged in the door.

"Do we even have a life?" Beth said, catching part of the conversation as she entered the room. "I mean. This job seems to consume all my time."

"You are so right, Beth," Vicky added. "Ernie, I bet you never think about this place after you are off work."

"If you only knew," Ernie said quietly.

Eleanor Porter dragged herself in at that moment. After greeting the others, she plopped down on one of the chairs by what passed as a conference table and slurped her coffee like a vampire sucking life-giving blood.

"Come on, El. Aren't you supposed to be on sick leave? I thought Cletus told you to take a full week off. Why are you back in here so soon? You are going to make yourself sick, really sick. A few days off won't do it for you, Honey. You need to rest," lectured Ernie, good-naturedly.

Eleanor did look worn out. She was sixty years old and slowed already by old injuries in her back and knees, the result of a serious car accident years ago. Most would say she looked older than her years. Her once blonde hair was now heavily streaked with grey and her face was lined with wrinkles. She had put on some pounds and seemed to labor just moving around the office. And now, she was trying to fight off a sinus infection that had dogged her for over two weeks.

But Eleanor was a trooper. She had been working in all phases of child welfare for thirty-eight years. Every one of her peers respected her for her dedication, vast storehouse of knowledge, and experience. El held a Masters Degree in Social Work. After a long time in foster care and adoptions, she switched to investigations approximately nine years ago. She had investigated hundreds of cases over the years, many the most difficult ones. She could handle anything in court and was highly respected or even feared by attorneys representing the opposing side. The very first thing attorneys would try in court was to discredit the investigator for lack of training and experience. They could not even attempt that tactic when Eleanor was testifying. The agency often asked her to handle high profile cases, putting the best foot forward so to speak, because of her impeccable credentials.

"I have court today, and I feel like crap," Eleanor moaned. "I think I'd better go see a doctor. Is Cletus in yet? I need to go over a few things with him."

"What hearing do you have, El?" asked Beth, knowing full well that her colleague was probably very ill but came in anyway because of the court involvement.

"Do you remember that big car dealer who was arrested for child rape?"

"Sure," Beth said. "How could we forget that one? Darnell Rogers-Smithson, the big wheel business man who had sex with his daughter's best friend, right?"

"That's the one. It went to Circuit Court as a criminal matter but Darnell Rogers-Smithson called in two high-powered attorneys and eventually he got off because of a technicality. His attorneys alleged in pretrial motions that there was a break in the chain of evidence. From what I understand, there was none, but somehow they were able to sell the idea that a break occurred to the judge. She ruled in Rogers-Smithson's favor. As a result the prosecution could not use the results of the rape kit and his DNA from the vaginal swipe. They tried the case anyway and lost. The victim was great on the stand. But that awful man was acquitted anyway."

"Now we are going to try to get him on child sexual abuse in the juvenile section of the Circuit Court. It's a little like going after O.J. Simpson in civil court because he was acquitted in criminal court."

"Oh, I remember that case," said Vicky. "Wasn't the victim staying with him and his wife while her parents cruised the Greek Isles for a month?"

"Yes. And since he was responsible for the child at the time of the rape, he is guilty of child sexual abuse. However, he has a new team of attorneys challenging our assertion that he was in an adult caretaker role at the time of the incident. As you know, if an adult is not in a caretaker role, they cannot be accused of abuse, neglect or anything in the statutes regarding dependent children," Eleanor said.

"They are going after the caretaker section of the law itself. His attorneys will challenge the caretaker statute in several different ways including the assertion that the caretaker role is vaguely written and thus unenforceable in relationship to this dependency case. I assume they will also assert that the wife was the caretaker, and not him."

"Remember the victim was fourteen at the time, a felony. That fellow ought to be serving a long prison sentence right now. Can you believe that happened nearly two years ago? He may have raped several other girls by now," Eleanor continued.

"El, it always amazes me how big bucks and some political capital can push back so hard," said Beth.

She knew full well that the outcome of El's case was not certain at all. She had been around long enough not to take anything for granted.

"You have a strong case, don't you?" asked Vicky.

"I think so and so do our attorneys. We should be able to use the physical evidence in the dependency proceedings even though it was rejected in the criminal trial. If not, the victim and her mother will testify as well as nurses and counselors that helped pull her back together. The kid was raped, Beth. And she is going to make one strong witness against that creep. But, you never know. I sure don't feel confident about it. I smell a rat!" answered El.

"I know what you mean," Beth almost whispered.

"Come on girls." offered Ernie. "Let's not borrow trouble. Everyone here works very hard to do the very best they can, and that sure applies to the three of you. El, it will not be your fault if this case does not go our way. So, put a smile on that face, get yourself that doctor's appointment that you should have taken care of days ago, and relax. What will be will be."

Later that afternoon, the case against Darnell Rogers-Smithson was withdrawn. Not a word of explanation was forthcoming. The Florida Department of Children's Services just dropped the case. It was months later that the reason became known. The law was quietly rewritten to strengthen the definition of a caretaker, an adult other than the parent who had taken responsibility for a child. The powers at be pulled the case because they feared that hundreds of old cases involving an abusing caretaker other than the parent would have to tossed out or reheard. All that made sense to the attorneys. Unfortunately it did not make any sense to the now sixteen-year old victim. She fled the courtroom sobbing hysterically while her broken mother, who seemed lost and exhausted, stumbled blankly on behind her. Eventually the girl slid into depression, with unresolved issues and fears.

With her on that slide was one, Eleanor Porter.

Chapter 11

The next morning Cletus assigned new investigations to all of the caseworkers as soon as they walked in the door, with the exception of Eleanor who was back on sick leave.

"I hope you gave me something interesting, Cletus," Vickie said. "I have had four unfounded cases in a row. I am getting a little tired of ex-husbands or neighbors trying to use child abuse as a weapon to get at Mom for one reason or another. We do have a false reporting law, don't we? Why on earth don't we use it now and then," Vickie asked, although no one bothered to answer.

Beth was assigned a child neglect report on a family living north of town in the more rural part of Escambia County. Normally one staff member handled the north end but that turf had belonged to the man who had been in the now vacant position.

The report had come in on the afternoon of the previous day but because of the nature of the complaint, it was not coded immediate. The staff had twenty-four hours in which to respond if the children were not in immediate danger.

Beth read over the report quickly. Ernie had already made a note that there was a prior complaint on the family in the computer's database. It was a similar report closed as unfounded four months earlier. It was alleged that twin boys were not being properly supervised. The new one contained the same allegation but added that the father had built a fence around the house that might be electrified.

Beth found the home at the end of a dirt road. She crossed a cattle gate and drove to the front of the place, an older farmhouse in need of paint but otherwise in good repair. She immediately noticed the fence. It was made of numerous strands of wire looped and strung between metal T bars that had been pounded into the ground. It encircled the entire house and looked totally out of place, almost like wire strung around a jail. It was located too close to the house. What appeared to be the remains of a more normal fence were in evidence. A few old poles still marked the line where a wooden fence had once stood.

Beth got out of the car and walked to the gate. She immediately noticed the two boys sitting on the ground playing with Matchbox cars near the front porch. They were staring at her. She warmly greeted the pair, perfectly gorgeous little towheads with freckled noses and bright smiles on their faces. They called out sweetly to her to come on in.

As soon as she placed her hand on the gate, she remembered that the complaint had alleged that the fence might be electrified. It was. There was an audible snap as the shock smacked her hand followed by a convulsion that shook her whole body. She just knew she had wet her pants. But, in truth, there was no injury. However, she soon found one. The two little angels were now rolling around on the ground laughing hysterically.

It was then that she noticed a small hand written note taped to the fence that instructed visitors to turn off the power by the tree before entering. She turned rapidly, found the switch, and gingerly touched the gate again to open it. She swung it open with half a mind to snatch up the two little devils when she heard a woeful cry from someone in the house.

"Noooooo!"

But it was too late. As soon as the gate was open the two boys rushed past her and took off in two different directions. At the same moment, a frantic woman charged out the door of the house and ran by Beth hollering for her to get the one in a blue shirt. Beth got the picture immediately and sped after the one so identified while the woman tore off after the other.

Beth was amazed how fast her quarry was, but she closed ground quickly flying through a field of hay like Emmett Smith, free in the secondary. She grabbed him just short of the end of the field, close to the woods.

"Ow! Ow!" screamed the kid, flopping around like a fish out of water while Beth struggled to secure her hold on him. As it turned out, she got him in a kind of bear-hug facing her. She simple held on as the child wiggled and squirmed to get free. But in so doing, the boy somehow got his hand inside her shirt, popping two buttons in the process. Then, like a teen on a hot date, he managed to plunge his little hand right down into her bra. There he found something protruding which he could pinch with his stubby fingers and so he went ahead and did just that.

"Ow! Ow!" screamed the investigator as she dropped her hold on him and wrenched his pincher off of her nipple. Sensing he was free of her, the little booger flew off again, leaving Beth in the dust.

The boy made straight for a large tree on the edge of the woods with Beth hot on his heels. Like a squirrel being chased by a dog, the kid simply flew up the tree effortlessly. While she watched helplessly panting from below, he climbed higher and higher until he made it to the upper-most branches.

Then she heard the woman calling out to her. The other son was racing right toward the same tree with the mother in hot pursuit. Beth moved to intercept him, her karate trained body ready to strike out and take him down. The boy swerved at the very last second, like a mongoose zipping away from the cobra's strike. She managed to get one hand on the neck of his shirt but fell down as he shrugged the garment right off his head and let her keep it. As she rolled quickly to try to grab him again, he jumped on the tree and followed his brother up into the safety of the highest limbs.

The women stood below and watched them for a bit. They didn't even bother to call up to them and ask them to climb down. That seemed to be a total waste of time. It had been a game and the unholy pair had won. The boys grinned down at them like twin Cheshire cats, side by side, enjoying the moment. They did not taunt or tease the women, but their safe perch high out of reach tormented them both, no less for one than the other.

"Hi," Beth said weakly to her companion, who was still winded.

"You must be Mrs. Hayes. Believe it or not, I'm from the child welfare agency. I think you had a visit from us once before. Anyway, we received a report about your fence. I guess I already know why you have one."

"Yes," Mrs. Hayes whispered. "We have a very hard time with them. I really don't know what to do anymore. I knew that fence was not right but it did work for a while. Do you think you could help us?"

"I really don't know, Mrs. Hayes, but I will certainly try."

"What do we do now?" Beth asked.

"I'll call Seymore. He's a welder and works just a short distance from here. He can help us," Mrs. Hayes offered.

"Do we just leave them here?" Beth queried, with more than a little concern in her voice.

"Yes, they will stay up there for most of the day, particularly if we watch them," Mrs. Hayes replied.

"Come on back to the house, I will get you something to drink."

Mr. Seymore Hayes arrived shortly thereafter. He was tall and thin, dressed all in black like Johnny Cash. His features were sharp and angular. His eyes blazed with anger as he passed right by her without saying a word and stomped into his house. Beth could sense that things may go from bad to worse right away. Her instincts were correct. Mr. Hayes went straight into the house and came out with an air rifle.

"Whoa there!" cried Beth. "I'm an investigator with the Department Of Children's Services. I can't allow you to shoot those boys," she said with great alarm.

Mr. Hayes didn't even bother to recognize her presence. He simple marched straight on a beeline for a particular tree on the other side of the hay field. Beth scooted after him with the Mrs. in tow all the while warning and threatening him if he should do what he damn well intended to do.

When he reached the bottom of the tree, he threw the gun up and sighted in on his sons.

"Get down here now. Don't make me shoot you. You understand," he growled.

Beth could no longer take it. She moved swiftly to Mr. Hayes and deftly disarmed him. He jumped back from her with a surprised look on his face as if this woman had worked some kind of magic. In a way she had.

"What in the name of God?" he stammered.

"Please, Mr. Hayes," Beth began. "I simply can't let you shoot those boys. I don't have arrest powers, but I could have you arrested for that. My job is to protect children. Let's calm down and come up with another solution."

"Listen lady. My wife and I have tried every thing. The boys get plumb wild. I thought you understood that by now. You figure it out. I'll leave the gun here. Let me know if you change your mind," Seymore Hayes said with great patience.

Then he turned and walked back to his house. Mrs. Hayes reminded Beth that the boys would not move if they were watched and hurried off to join her husband.

"Geez!" Beth said to herself. Then she tried begging. She called up to the boys and gently asked them to come down. They answered her with derisive giggles.

She sat down and racked her brain. Then she hit upon a perfect solution. She pulled her cell phone out of her pocket and dialed 911.

She was still stewing over the fact that she was lectured by the 911operator about using the emergency line for a non emergency, not to mention the reception she had been given when she called the local fire house. The fireman who answered the phone had greeted her with heehaws and chuckles until she blessed out the man and reminded him that he would think nothing of it if a damn cat were stuck up a tree.

Soon the fire truck arrived at the house. Beth watched as Mr. Hayes came out of the house and visited with the men who drove it. They talked for what seemed like ten minutes or more while she waited, stewing about it. She could hear them laugh even at the distance between house and tree. Finally the two firemen got in and cranked up the truck. Slowly they made their way out to her on a circuitous route along the tree line so as not to leave tracks through the hay. Good thing it's no emergency, she reminded herself.

"Hello Missy," said the driver, an old man, probably 70, with a plump beer belly partially covered with a stained blue work shirt and sporting a tan pair of brush pants held up with suspenders. He was obviously the leader of the pair as the other fellow was just a kid.

"I'm Deputy Chief Treadway. Hear you have a little problem," he said with a condescending grin on his face. "We'll get those boys down for you. Don't you worry your pretty little head over it any more. We'll get those boys down here right quick."

It was right then and there that Beth remembered that her blouse was torn and hanging open. Deputy Chief Treadway was talking directly to her breasts. His eyes were fixed on her chest all the while he was yammering away. She quickly looked down. To her horror she discovered that her pretty black bra was almost totally uncovered and struggling mightily to hold her bosom in place. She looked every bit like the obligatory woman on the cover of all Harlequin Romances, full, heaving bodice revealed for the pleasure of a looming lover.

Damn, she mouthed silently as she struggled to pull and push things here and there to gain some semblance of modesty.

After enjoying her efforts for a moment, the chief turned to the other man and told him to get the fire hose off the truck.

"Yep, we'll have those urchins down here quick," he announced.

"What? You aren't going to blast them out of the tree with water are you?" Beth shouted.

"Why sure. That's what we do with cats."

"Turn that damn pump off!" Beth demanded.

"Those aren't cats up there! The boys could lose their grip and fall the whole way down that tree. Sir, you could easily hurt them badly and you know it! I should call the police right now!" Beth said angrily.

"Now pack up your just so special little ole fire man's truck and get out of here!" she barked.

"OK Missy. We were just trying to help," the old man cooed sweetly.

Beth walked away and tried to think as the men prepared to leave. She was about as frustrated as she could get. She concluded that she would climb the tree herself and somehow talk the boys down.

Just then she heard three pops from the BB gun.

"Now you get down here before I put one in your eyes." the chief bellowed with serious authority.

Beth snapped her head around and stood transfixed. She watched inconceivably as the two boys hurriedly scampered back down to the ground and then hurried off on a straight line across the hay field to their father.

Slowly she walked over to Deputy Chief Treadway.

"I'm going to file a report with the police," she said.

"That is assault and you know it."

"Well, Missy, you go ahead and do that if you want. I know all the deputies who work at the sub-station up here. I think I can work something out. So do your duty. I'm sure that will make you feel real proud of yourself. But before you put your butt in that Mustang and drive on back to Pensacola, I need to get something off my chest."

"You people sure take the cake. You think you know everything there is to know about children. I bet you aren't even married. Well, we aren't so dumb out here. We have raised a child or two. Seymore knew what he was doing, and you stopped him. Even though he is the parent, you tell him what he can and can't do. According to you folks he is not supposed to lay a finger on those babies, right?"

"I pop the boys and what's the harm?" the old fireman continued. "I'm truly sorry I violated YOUR standards for getting children to behave? But to tell you the truth, if need be, I'll be doing it again."

"Hold on a second Mr.," Beth snapped. "Don't talk to me like I'm some kind of a child. I don't tell you how to put out your little brush fires. I don't walk around putting you down when you split your hoses and someone's house burns down either. There are two sides to my story, and I want you to hear me out. If you care about the Hayes' and their kids, follow me over to the house."

"Ok, sister," the chief said steaming a little. "I'll take you up on that."

Soon Beth had Mr. and Mrs. Hayes and the two firemen together in the front yard.

"First of all, we don't do anything that's not in state law. If you guys have a problem with the law, see your local representatives. Second, we are just like firemen. We roll when we are called. Someone has to file a report," Beth explained.

"Someone living out here is concerned about these boys and by law I cannot and will not tell you who that is. The names are confidential. Got that. But let's get back to the point. The report indicated that Mr. Hayes might be using an electric fence to pen the boys up. I came out here and guess what? It's true. That fence is dangerous too. I know because I touched the darn thing by accident, and it really hurt. I know that you are getting desperate Mr. Hayes, but that is way over the top and out of line."

"And as for you, Mr. Treadway," she said, now on a roll with some anger, "shooting the boys with a BB rifle was stupid. If you shot me on purpose, you would be arrested for assault. You know that. Those boys could have panicked and fallen. Or a slight ricochet could have taken an eye out. Give me a break!"

"Let's talk about how we got to this place."

"Well," said Seymore Hayes. "I was reported about six months ago because I was supposedly disciplining them too harshly. You folks don't want us to touch them and so I don't."

"Did someone actually tell you not to touch them?" Beth asked.

"No, not in so many words. But everyone knows you folks will come to call if we do and eventually take the children away."

"Bull hockey!" fumed Beth.

"Mr. Hayes, listen to me and listen good. We don't take children from their parents unless something very serious is going on. And even then a judge ultimately decides in court, not us."

"I urge both of you to discipline those boys. They are wild as colts and need to be reined in. You need to cramp down on them hard, right now. Sit down together and agree on a plan. But, do not hurt them! DO NOT use a belt or a razor strap or a board or an electric cord or anything else like that. You may paddle them if you think that will help. Use an open hand on the butt. There are better things you can try like taking away things they want if they act out. You might need to throw away those matchbox toys for example. Whatever. You and your wife do what you need to do short of injuring those boys, and you will have no problem with us. Do you understand me?"

Mr. Hayes was taken aback by the angry response he had provoked from the woman who stood before him. He quickly nodded in agreement. Mrs. Hayes said nothing but liked what this gal had to say.

Beth continued, now a little calmer, "By the way, remember to have some fun with them too. I think they are bored out of their minds. Try climbing the tree with them once in awhile. Throw a ball around. Plant a garden and get them to help. Get a big dog or some goats and put them in charge of looking after them. I think they would be thrilled. If absolutely nothing seems to work I'd take a chainsaw to that tree."

"A dog's not a bad idea," Mr. Hayes said with some enthusiasm.

"I'm going to close this case as indicated for child endangerment. But, I will explain that you meant no harm and no further services are required at this time. I believe that you can handle your boys. If not, call the number on this card and ask to speak to a Protective Services worker. They will try to get you some help with discipline on a volunteer basis."

"You better get rid of that fence though. Promise me! It makes your home look like a prison camp or something. Besides, whoever called us will probably be watching and call again. If you don't remove it, I'll have to come back and then we will have to get serious."

"I hate that thing too. It bit me twice. I asked Seymore not to do it in the first place," Mrs. Hayes chimed in.

"I should have taken it down before I guess," Seymore Hayes said, almost apologetically.

"Chief, as you say, no harm was done. No harm, no foul, I guess. I won't file a police report. But, please, have some respect for what we do just as we have respect for firemen. And I sure wish you could come off that "Missy" business. It's like me calling you "Junior" or something. Come visit me at the office some day, and I'll show you around. We aren't a bunch of old ladies in stuffed shirts."

"I may take you up on that invitation, Miss er..."

"Just call me Beth."

"Ok, Beth. I do need to tell you one thing though," said Deputy Chief Treadway. "You aren't an old lady. But that shirt of yours really is stuffed. It sure makes an old man smile though."

They all laughed. After giving the parents some more ideas to help discipline and occupy the children, Beth said her goodbyes. She piled back into her Mustang and made tracks. What a morning she said to herself. Please, can't I have a simple little case once in awhile, she mused. Then with sunglasses cocked in place and the rock station blasting in her ears, full-bore, she drove headlong back to the office.

Chapter 12

About the same time that Beth was chasing after the twins at the Hayes' place, a grizzly discovery was made back in the city. A woman out walking her dog in a neighborhood on a side street off of Old Palafox smelled a foul odor. The stench seemed to be coming from a notorious house on her street. The place was a mess. It seemed to exceed the definition of an eyesore in comparison to the other modest homes on the street.

There had been scant mowing or yard work done for years. Litter and other rusty trash lay tangled in weeds and overgrown shrubs. The house itself seemed to be moments away from simply crashing down under its own weight. The only painting or repair done in decades was a patched roof job. A hurricane had toppled a tree that punched a hole in the roof. Mennonites who traveled into the area to help poor folks re-roof their homes cut down the tree and completed a partial replacement of the roof for the occupant. They even stayed over a day to clean the yard as best they could, probably forestalling for a time the legal condemnation of the property. The woman remembered thinking it would never have been repaired at all if those good folks had not shown up from somewhere near Century, Florida.

There were odors from that particular place before, but not like this. Therefore the neighbor called 911 to report it. She specified that it smelled like there may be something dead in the house. The veteran patrol officer who responded could see the body of a woman lying in a bed through a tear in a curtain that hung in a bedroom window. There was blood splattered everywhere. He drew back in horror but managed to recover and see to his work. He retreated excitedly, called for his patrol sergeant, and started hanging crime scene tape. There was no question about foul play.

The neighbor who had made the 911 call approached the officer. He told her that she was correct about the odor but did not mention anything else. She just assumed that the woman died of natural causes that somehow reflected her rather poor standard of living. But she did say that there were rumors that she was a prostitute. Perhaps she died of an overdose of drugs. The savy cop grunted an acknowledgement but did not reveal that the victim's throat had been cut, ear-to-ear.

His sergeant arrived soon thereafter, checked out the gruesome scene through the bedroom window, and immediately called dispatch to alert the medical examiner's office, the crime scene technicians, and a team of investigators from the unit that usually worked crimes against persons cases

Ed Kambler, a medical examiner investigator, arrived next soon followed by two crime scene investigators. They all spoke with the sergeant briefly then entered the house.

Soon two men drove up and slowly dragged themselves out of their unmarked car. One, looking like a college BMOC, was wearing a sharp blue blazer and grey slacks. The other, a huge hulking mass of a man, was clad in a vintage green and white checked sport coat and a pair of rumpled brown slacks. The two sauntered over to the sergeant and received their briefing. In summing up, he told them to be sure to talk with the 911 caller who was sitting on her porch across the street. The new arrivals approached the house but did not enter. The one signaled the other, taking notice of the odor with just a wrinkle of the nose. Then the investigators stopped and talked with the officer that had discovered the body. This fellow clued them in with respect to the cause of death. To prove the point, he took them behind the house and showed them his peep-hole in the curtain.

The detectives took turns checking out what they could see from their limited vantage point. The bed was only a foot or two away from the curtain but Ed Kambler was standing right in front of them taking pictures. Even so, they got a good impression that the murder had been bloody. They could see a few droplets on the window itself and elsewhere in their line of sight, a distance from the body itself.

Ed suddenly moved away while the sharp dresser was peering into the room. Totally unprepared for the carnage, he gasped as almost all of his senses were suddenly overpowered. He froze like a deer in the glow of headlights and stared at the stink and gore, unable to break away. The killer had been brutal. Images of someone butchering the victim flashed through his mind while his stomach turned and bile welled up in his throat. Finally he broke with his morbid fascination, turned, walked a few paces away, and hurled the contents of his stomach into the weeds.

As he wiped his mouth with a hanky, he steeled himself so that he would never react that way again. It was not that he hadn't seen murder victims before, as he had many times since transferring to the crimes against persons unit three years ago. It was simply the one bloody scene that would change things. With one bout of nausea he shed a certain innocence that all cops must jettison in time if they are to survive on the streets.

The other cop quickly replaced his partner at the window. With much more experience with foul murder scenes he looked upon the decomposing victim without a trace that it bothered him in the least. But, deep down in his soul where such visages take their toll, another notch was carved next to dozens of others. He winched ever so slightly at the pain and would bare the accumulating scars forever.

Then they went back to the street. First they worked the small crowd of on-lookers that had gathered. Next they visited with the woman on her porch. Finally they started knocking on doors. They were fishing. They were fishing for information about the victim and activity around the house in recent days.

After the crime-scene team had photographed the scene, taken swabs and fingerprints, and gathered what evidence they could in the bedroom, work started in the rest of the place. One stayed inside while the other came out to nose around outside. He badly wanted a cigarette, and he didn't even smoke.

This did not go unnoticed by the two investigators, although they were several doors down from the crime scene. They converged on this guy asking for more details about the inside of the house. He started off by giving them all he knew of the victim's identifying information. Her name was Milly McCanless, age thirty-nine. He noted that her pocket book was on a dresser by the bed. An expired driver's license and a few dollar bills were clearly visible within it. He was able to give them a few other good observations that included the fact that she was probably drunk and having sex just before she was killed. Then he added one more thing.

"It's damn filthy in there. If you move something, you stir up roaches. It looks like the gal never picked up anything. There is junk all over, most of it just ordinary trash."

Just as they were about to wrap up that conversation, the other crime scene investigator called out to them from the front door.

"Hey Jack. Loomis. You guys can come in now. Thanks for being patient. It is so crowded in that bedroom. When you are done looking around in there, come see me. I have something I want to show you off the hall," she said.

"Thanks, Nannette," Jack responded. "We'll be right in."

The detectives jumped to, popped on some gloves, and headed to the front door. After entering the dwelling, they went straight to the bedroom. Outside the door they chatted with Ed Kambler for a while. He confirmed the obvious in regard the cause of death and gave them an estimate of the time of death as well.

"Your bad guy has a jump on you guys. She has been cooking for some time," he said. "I'd guess three days at least. Maybe a little more. Better look for someone who was ticked off with this poor gal. He sure did a number on her throat."

Ed excused himself and moved on giving the detectives a chance to do their thing. They both stood beside the bed and took a very close look at the victim, recording a mental picture of every detail. Then they turned and spent some time looking closely at everything in the room including the contents of the purse, taking notes as they worked.

Next they found the crime-scene investigator who had called out to them. She was working in a small room off the hall. She had discovered a crib. It was made up with a single, fitted sheet. In one corner of the bed a green, plush hippo lay staring longingly into space as if bereaved and lonely.

"I always had a blanket for my boys when they were still in the crib. If nothing else they hugged it while sucking their thumbs," said Nannette. "There is none here, but I can see what looks like pink lint on the sheet in several places."

"I don't want to complicate this, but there was a child here," she added solemnly.

Jack Mulkey and his partner Loomis were easily convinced. When they first entered the room, Loomis had silently signaled Jack to look to his left with an exaggerated nod of his head. There were lots of baby clothes strewn about. More to the point, Loomis had spotted a baby bottle half filled with formula on a small table and several dirty diapers in a trashcan. Their investigation would now include a quiet search for another victim.

Further inspection by the cops revealed something else of note. There was an unusual uncluttered area around a decent looking chair in what once was a living room. The chair faced a working TV and was sided by a solid oak table. On the table there was a large Hardies Coca Cola cup that contained several inches of dark liquid and numerous soggy Winston cigarette butts. On the floor nearby Jack spotted a Hardies bag. Opening it carefully they found two sandwich wrappers, a fry box, and numerous napkins. There had been no other evidence of smoking in the place, not even a lighter. Loomis guessed that the killer or someone else had sat there for at least two hours near the time of the murder.

The detectives made a point to tell Nannette to collect the cup and bag.

"You guys are something else," she said with a smile in her voice. "I was on it. Get your butts out of here and let me do my job. I assume you will want a full written analysis of the entire scene by 5:00 this afternoon, right?"

"Well," Loomis bellowed in his deep baritone voice. "Those CSI guys in Vegas get DNA results and everything else done in minutes. We still don't know why y'all have to be so slow."

"We're just sorry I guess," Nannette fired back. "But do consider this, my friends. Without us you can't get the first conviction. So go on. After we figure out who done it, we'll call you so you can be heroes and make an arrest. Catch a few headlines and such."

"Umm," moaned Loomis as if he had taken a direct punch to the stomach. "You hit below the belt," he said with a laugh.

They thanked Nannette for the help, reminded Ed they needed a solid time of death when he was finished at the lab, and then got out of there. Splitting up they slowly circled the house looking for any sign of a baby, fibers, toys, something out of the ordinary, or a place to dump a helpless child. They met in the alley behind the house then separated again, one going east, the other west. As they walked they cautiously opened every trashcan they could find. There was little to see. The garbage had no doubt been picked up recently.

Both familiar with crimes against persons and homicide cases in particular, they had already formulated solid ideas about what had occurred there. From what they had gathered, they came to believe that the murderer had been a close associate of the victim. The killing had been personal. The victim had been rather brutally slain, close up and with a very sharp bladed weapon. Also a child was probably taken, perhaps by the father who was rescuing the child from the squalor that defined the victim's lifestyle.

Jack Mulkey had been a cop for several months short of seven years. At the age of twenty-eight he still looked like a college boy. He was six feet tall, built like a star athlete, and as handsome as a jaybird. He sported curly, sandy brown hair, light hazel eyes, and a chiseled chin that gave him an instant air of confidence and masculinity. In addition Jack was intelligent, very well spoken, and committed. He had recently received a B.A. in Criminal Justice at the University of West Florida. The Sheriff often put him on camera for press releases and liked to have him present for community good will campaigns.

As an investigator, Mulk, as he was tagged by his partner, was known to be intuitive, decisive, and accurate in analyzing information. But, he disdained what he called grunt work and would often zone out quickly when he thought he was wasting his time. In addition he was neither street wise nor particularly tough. Some of the other cops called him "pretty boy" behind his back. Because Jack was unmarried and did not seem to be interested in women, one or two others called him worse.

He and Loomis had hit it off from day one. Both never blinked when each met his new partner. Perhaps they knew instinctively that they would make one hell of a good team. They truly complimented each other. In addition Loomis, who looked like a thug in his ill-fitting clothes, silenced the whispers about Jack without saying a word. Conversely, Jack's ready acceptance of his partner helped Loomis make a smooth adjustment to the squad, the courts, and the community.

The first thing, the very first thing one recognized about Arthur Windell Loomis was the fact that he was a light skinned biracial redhead with a ton of freckles. Some thought he was albino. Growing up on the mean streets of the Big Easy was hard for any kid but well nigh impossible for him. His unusual face and his flaming red hair provoked an immediate negative reaction from almost everyone save close family members and a few friends. But Loomis survived. He survived by breaking open the faces of those who made fun of his. Also he developed a keen understanding of right from wrong that most street kids blurred at their convenience. He knew that those who tormented and beat him were wrong. Conversely punishing those who did, felt good. Very good indeed!

Loomis had been a cop all his life. He battled for almost nine years on the rugged streets of New Orleans. There he had been shot a total of four times and stabbed twice. In addition he had duked it out with the bad guys numerous times, suffering a litany of injuries including a smashed nose that he wore permanently on his scared face. A drunken tire salesman from Utah had provided the facial during Mardi Gras. He simply walked up beside Loomis and blind-sided him with an empty beer bottle, no real harm intended.

After getting run out of the Big Easy for banging the wife of a local politico, Loomis was immediately picked up by the Memphis P.D. where his particularly hard, albeit decidedly crooked, nose was welcomed. Here he was appreciated for what he was, a tough, determined cop who took no uninjured prisoners. A keen intelligence that belied his looks and his rugged disposition soon won him the reputation as the top detective on the Memphis squad.

He thought he would retire to Pensacola after serving a total of twenty-one years in the two big cities, thinking he could take it easy in the sunshine. But it was not three weeks before he signed on with the Escambia County Sheriff's Department. Tired of breaking in young rookie cops, the Sheriff jumped at the chance to snag an experienced veteran. He offered him an investigator position immediately although Loomis had been hooked at "hello." With two years under his belt in Escambia County, Loomis was now a twenty-three year veteran of the war on crime.

At the age of 44, Loomis was the equivalent of the nasty old house where the slain woman had been found. He always looked like he had slept in his clothes, rumpled and crumpled like a large ball of discarded wrapping paper. He was rough around the edges, and to people who did not know him he always seemed to be one step away from violence. Even his graveled, cigarette damaged, low register voice made others pause. In comparison he would have made Lt. Norman Buntz from Hill Street Blues look like a choir boy.

Loomis was six foot five and well over 250 pounds. Massively built. He was somewhat overweight and out of shape. Smoked like a burning tire. But no one messed with him. His unusual skin, coupled with his crimson facial scars gave him the look of something alien, a threatening presence that frightened most women and children and made tough guys shiver. Often while effortlessly playing the bad cop next to Jack's good cop, the pair was able to snag information and statements that others could not.

Now, before leaving the neighborhood the detectives started in on their murder investigation in earnest by going door to door. They already had one hot tip from a bystander. The victim was occasionally seen in the company of a short dark haired man who drove a rusty blue or dark green Impala. They hoped for something more. At the last house on the block, they got it. A woman said they needed to talk to the boy who babysat for the victim. She knew his name and address, as she had used his services as well.

"Mulk, how sweet is that?" Loomis growled as they piled into their car and headed straight to the babysitters house.

Unfortunately they couldn't connect with their witness. The boy's father answered the door and became alarmed. He understood they were investigating the murder of the woman who had hired his boy to baby-sit. The father insisted that he be present when the boy was interviewed. The man was headed off for the three to eleven shift at a local manufacturing plant. He promised to bring his son to the Sheriff's Department and meet with the officers early in the morning.

They went back to their office and worked the computer trying to locate an older model Impala that was registered in the area. They got a bunch of hits on the car search, more than they had anticipated. They spent almost the entire evening running down cars and burning up the phone lines.

The press had the murder story but nothing on the missing baby. After conferring with Lt. Steve Orlando, their boss, they decided to ask for public help in locating the child. Before leaving for the night they did some groundwork for a press conference the next day.

Chapter 13

The central abuse and neglect hotline based in Tallahassee, Florida received a call from a woman Saturday morning indicating that she needed to talk to Bill Kraznasky as soon as possible, adding that it was important. She explained that she had been the subject of a report a few months ago. Bill had come out to see her. He had closed the matter as unfounded, a nasty joke or an attempt to harass the woman for one reason or another, but he had told her to call him if she had any more problems. It was a standard line he used all the time. In this situation there was no reason to say it at all. There was nothing to investigate. She didn't even have a child.

Registry staff checked the central computer record and found the complaint. Bill was listed as the investigator. Since the message rang true they alerted the on call investigator on duty in Pensacola. Such calls were not logged on the computer and could be handled as the local staff wished. The on call worker in Pensacola was not from Cletus' unit but knew Bill well. She decided that Bill might want to know. He could get involved again or totally ignore the call if he chose. She found his home phone number and dialed him up.

Mr. Bill was still lulling around in bed at 9:00 A.M when he got the message. Damn, he thought. Bessie? I wonder what's going on? But, he had no plans really other than a night on the town later with several of his friends. So, he slowly got up and dressed before downing a huge bowl of cold cereal, all the while thinking of the woman he had met months before.

Bessie Bunyon was huge, almost six feet tall and large boned. Everything about her was big including her head, hands, and feet. Her given age was twenty-seven although Bill felt that she looked a little younger than that. She wore her brown wavy hair too short and that alone coupled with a strong face and prominent chin gave her a distinctly masculine appearance. But, as he remembered she was actually very much a woman, very sweet and even a little flirtatious. He recalled that she dressed to accent her bust line wearing a low cut V neck top which didn't help too much given that her size overshadowed the attempt at femininity. In truth he remembered feeling a little sorry for her. She lived with her grandfather out in the country and seemed to be isolated and perhaps without friends.

Bill phoned Bessie and told her he could be there by 11:00 A.M.

He arrived at her rural home in the vicinity of McDavid at the appointed hour. When he knocked on the door, Bessie opened it sporting that same low cut top. He wondered for a moment if she owned any others. They exchanged small talk as she invited him in and then ushered him to a huge couch, asked him to sit, and when he did, sat down beside him.

"I'm curious, Bessie," he said. "What's on your mind?" Bill asked, probing directly for whatever prompted her to call.

"Why yes, Bill," she answered. "I need your help."

"Is someone threatening to file another false report?" Bill guessed.

"No," she said demurely.

"Let me get you something to drink," Bessie said, suddenly changing the subject. And in the same instant she rose and walked out of the living room and disappeared. Bill was able to manage a partial word or two in protest, but Bessie just went on as if unhearing.

Bill sat looking around the room for several minutes. There was a framed picture of her grandfather on a table by the couch. He knew the old fellow as Ralph. He owned the house and paid all the bills. Then his eyes fell on her glass rabbit collection. He distinctly remembered it from before. Bessie had over twenty-five small glass rabbits that she proudly displayed in a glass display case that stood almost five feet high. It looked like she had added a few more. He rose to take a look at them. Several minutes passed and he was beginning to wonder where she was when she walked back into the room balancing two tall glasses, ice cubes tinkling softly, and two sandwiches on an old-fashioned beer tray.

"I knew you would be hungry," she announced, sitting down beside him.

"Oh, I already ate," he lied. "But a glass of water would be fine," Bill said, trying to be polite.

She placed the tray on an end table and handed him one of the glasses.

"I hope this will do," she responded.

Bill, truly thirsty, accepted the glass and took a deep draw. He almost choked as he instantaneously tried to spit out the vodka, and changing his mind to avoid spewing it all over the place, swallowed it like a dose of bad medicine.

"Damn!" Bill gasped.

"I'm sorry," Bessie said moving closer to him on the couch.

"I thought you would enjoy a little refreshment. Drink it slower. It is a family mix and is to be sipped leisurely and enjoyed over time. Have a bite of my egg salad too. I promise it is something special."

"Bessie," Bill croaked quietly, his voice now cracked and strained. Then lying again he added, "I have another appointment at 12:15. What is it that you want?"

Bessie responded by turning and embracing Bill, her bulk slamming him into the corner of the couch, effectively pinning him down. She didn't bother with any more small talk. She grabbed the bottom of her shirt and swiftly yanked it up and over her head, revealing a black bra two sizes too small overflowing with flesh. Then she grabbed her quarry by the scruff of his neck and slammed his face smack dab into her bosom.

"Mummer ugg!" Bill managed in a muffled attempt to scream, his voice disembodied and distant, his mouth and eyes totally slammed shut against her heaving breast.

Bessie released a guttural moan then strengthened her hold on Bill. Keeping him pinned, she shifted a little to one side and freed an arm. Then she plunged her hand into Bills crotch and cupped his privates. Unfortunately Bessie was not practiced in the art of lovemaking. She began a rigorous massage of Bill's package like she was scrubbing a bad stain off the kitchen floor. But sending shock waves of pain into his body was not the best way to arouse him.

Under his eyelids Bills eyes flared and widened like he had been brutally stabbed with a screwdriver. Another blunted howl emerged from his sealed lips like the echo of a terrible thunderstorm. Panicking he struggled and squirmed like a night crawler on a hook.

But the big woman held on. This was her time. This is what she dreamed of, and she was not to be denied. Like a black widow spider, she was going to mate, even if her lover was to die in the process.

Bill fought with his captor like a man possessed. This only seemed to convince her that her efforts to seduce him were working. Thus, she increased the speed of her already vigorous massage and stroked him with greater purpose. She was warmed by Bill's violent response as he thrashed and gurgled beneath her, mistaking his agony for throes of passion.

Tossing her head back in pleasure, Bessie began to enjoy a stirring in her loins.

Suffocating under the continued assault, Bill's energy began to wane. He could not breathe. He could not scream, and he could not move. Like a man about to drown, he welcomed the urge to just quietly slip away. He began to relax and to come to peace with the reality of his impending death. A warm sensation of peace enveloped him as he closed himself off from the pain.

Just then Bessie's fingers found his zipper and with one powerful yank, his fly was open. This invasion might have been welcomed under different circumstances, but now it terrorized him and sent a jolt of adrenaline surging through his body. With the fight response in full gear, Bill flexed and twisted his arms, legs, back, butt, and head in a fury. Somehow he managed to catch a breath. Now fueled even more for the fight, he worked his mouth open and bit poor Bessie hard on her tender breast.

Bessie screamed, jumped straight up off the couch and in so doing, pulled Bill like a tangled blanket part way to the floor. She seized the injured tit, snatching it free from the bra to examine her wound just as the grandfather walked in the front door.

Ralph Bunyon, near eighty with a great shock of silvery hair, bowed back and walking with a cane, still presented evidence of great height and girth. Bill found himself looking at him upside down though eyes blurred by tears. I guess Bessie didn't fall too far from the oak, he thought to himself. But it was the dog that grabbed most of his attention. Ralph clung desperately to a big black Lab mix with a leash. Even with a choker collar, the beast snarled and lunged at him.

"What in the name of Heaven?" Ralph roared.

The dog echoed Ralph's sentiment exactly by barking loudly and making one particularly brutal jump toward the home invader. The leap almost pulled Ralph's arm out of its socket and nearly toppled the old guy as it was. But he got command of his dog by belting it savagely over its head with his cane. It whimpered and shied, looking up sheepishly at his master as if totally ashamed. Then with one swift move Ralph turned and kicked the pooch out the door, leash and all, and slammed it behind him.

Ralph Bunyon closed the few feet between himself and Bill in a flash. Bill thought for a second that he was coming to help him up but the first blow of the cane sent that idea into thin air. Having now been fully whacked out of the doldrums, Bill found both energy and motivation to find still another way to avoid pain and injury. He quickly jettisoned himself the rest of the way off the couch onto his knees. Then like a cockroach he skittered across the living room floor toward the dining room. Ralph, in pursuit, chased after him in a fashion, swinging and missing like the last kid chosen for the team Unfortunately, one wild swing hit the glass-shelving unit and sent fragile bunnies flying everywhere.

Bessie had remained standing motionless until this very moment. She had been mortified by the fact that her sweet Poppa had caught her making love and may have laid eyes upon her partially naked breast. She had been totally embarrassed and ashamed. But, a new thought entered her mind that would restore her chastity.

"Get him Poppa!" she hollered. "He took advantage of me!" And as she continued to shout and encourage the old man, she set about trying to jam the loose boob back into her bra. She would have joined the fray but for the fact that it simply would not fit. Noticing that the boys were fully occupied, she decided to take the bra off and load up both girls again.

Bill had managed to find sanctuary under the dining room table without receiving another stripe from the cane. There, dodging sword-like thrusts of the stick by his pursuer, he fought for a second to figure out the best means of escape. Then he happened to see Bessie turn her back to take off her bra. A devilish idea hit him.

"Besseee!" he bellowed as loud as he could.

And just as he hoped, Bessie turned toward the dining room just as her grandfather shot around facing her. Both of them froze. Bessie in all her glory could do nothing but turn a bright crimson from head to toe. Her beloved Poppa stood transfixed, seeing the little girl he had raised as never before imagined.

Bill got lost for a second, admiring Bessie's unquestionably magnificent breasts, but managed to seize the opportunity to escape before it was lost. He crawled rapidly out from under the table and continued on his knees straight for the front door. Upon arrival he shot to his feet, opened it, jumped on to the porch, and slammed the door behind him.

Jogging quickly down the steps he enjoyed a wonderful sense of renewed freedom like a man released from prison until the dog roared out from under the porch to greet him. Barking like the place was afire, the dog approached, wild eyed and furious. Bill slowly backed off toward his car, the dog following, its jowls now dripping with saliva.

Suddenly the front door flew open and out plodded the old man with his cane. Bill froze by the car not sure if he could turn away from the dog long enough to open it and get in without a bite. Hurriedly Ralph Bunyon closed the distance between the two men. He raised the cane threatening as he neared.

"Go on Mullet!" he demanded.

Bill was not sure if Mr. Bunyon was addressing him or the dog. But it was the dog that answered by turning away from Bill and slinking slowly off, pausing only to pee on one of Bill's shiny chrome hubcaps. Now the two men faced each other once more. Bill decided he would have to beat up the old fellow to defend himself but down deep he wasn't exactly sure if he could. Conversely, he thought, considering the age of his combatant, could he live with himself if he did?

"Listen Mr. I want to apologize to you," said the old man softly and with contrition.

"Bessie told me it was her fault. She's hoping you will forgive her. She's lonely you know. She has never really had a date since high school."

Then Ralph Bunyon slowly turned and hobbled back to his house, head down, and defeated. But Bill, Mr. Bill to be exact, could not let it go like that. He called for the man to wait for him, joined him, and went back into the house. Mullet now waging his tail followed behind. They sat down and ate lunch together. Bessie's egg salad was perfect after all.

During the meal Bill chatted on like an old friend of the family. He asked the pair questions about their daily lives and made light conversation much like a preacher would during a routine visit. He spoke to the old man and his granddaughter in a positive and supportive manner, complimenting both at every opportunity. He was pleased that he did win a few smiles here and there.

After he helped her clear the table and said good-bye to Mr. Bunyon, Bill asked Bessie to accompany him to his car. There he made a more direct attempt to convince her that she had a great deal to offer and that there was someone out there for her.

"Bessie, I just want you to know that I'm not angry with you. I must admit that you scared me a little. You came on a bit strong. But that's not important. What is important is for you to keep your head up. You and I are not going to make the covers of glamour magazines. We can't match up with Hollywood's image of what a man or woman should look like. But don't ever think for a moment that we have nothing to offer. You are more attractive than you think. It's just that you need to gain a little experience dating and such. Out here you have little opportunity to meet anyone."

Bessie, hanging on every word Bill said, was silent for a moment. Then she responded.

"I did have a few dates in high school. One fellow was taken with me for awhile but he joined the Army, left and I never saw him again."

"See!" Bill replied, giving her limited dating history a positive twist.

"You can attract men. All you need to do is get out a little. Look around. There may be someone that you know that would love to hear from you."

"I'll try," she managed to say. But she didn't sound very convincing.

"There you go," he said in conclusion with a big encouraging grin on his face.

Bill decided to leave it at that. He wasn't sure if the little talk had helped Bessie at all. Yet as he climbed into his car she looked at him right in the eyes and thanked him.

As he wheeled his way home, Bill wondered if he had told Bessie the truth or simply flattered her. Down deep that same sense of sorrow for Bessie still haunted him. But, there was something about her, something he could not quite get a finger on. He wondered with a wry smile on his face if he would venture back out there again whether she called for him or not.

Chapter 14

The baby sitter was a tall skinny, pink faced teenage boy named Devin Knotts. His father had brought him in just as promised. At first the teen was tense and tightlipped. Jack and Loomis assumed that he was scared so they simply shot the bull with him and his Dad for a while until the kid became more at ease. When he did start talking, he proved to be extremely helpful.

He made it clear to the cops that he had only babysat there four or five times for the McCanless woman. He immediately figured out that she was probably worthless but he felt sorry for the baby. The child loved to be held and often simply fell asleep in his arms as he watched TV. He didn't like the filth and the damn roaches, but the money was good. The lad figured she couldn't get anyone else to go in that house. He didn't know the full name of the man who drove the blue Impala. The victim apparently just called him Dicky. Devin wasn't sure if Richard or Dick was his real name or not.

While the babysitter couldn't come up with a full name, he was certainly able to describe Dicky very, very, well.

Apparently, this guy was about five foot five at most. Kevin guessed he was probably forty-five or so. Obviously a man with pattern baldness, he was totally hairless in a large, near perfect round spot on top of his head. He kept the stringy black ring of hair that sprouted out around the side of his head, shoulder length, as if to compensate for the loss above. His tiny beady, mouse eyes were set too close together on a pock marked face and overshadowed by huge black eyebrows. In addition Dicky was round in the middle and stood on two rather skinny, short legs. Devin said the man reminded him of a freaky looking Danny Devito but rounder, like Tweedle Dee or Tweedle Dum.

The cops thanked Devin and his father for coming in, and they were both smiling like newlyweds at the reception, when they left. The kid might as well have served up the prime suspect on a silver platter. Both Jack and Loomis had seen the name Dicky before. It was not a given name. It wasn't even a sexy pet name McCanless might use to refer to her lover's little friend. No, it was a surname. The vehicle registration search revealed that one Purvis Dicky just happened to own and drive one sorry looking blue Impala on the same streets they did, right there in River City.

Following a short celebration, including backslaps and a resounding "Amen Brother!" from Loomis, the detectives pulled the records on Little Dicky, the nickname Loomis now began to call him derisively. He was a small time hoodlum with a large rap-sheet. His most recent arrest photo revealed the pattern baldness on the crown of his head, the stringy black hair, and the beady eyes just as the babysitter had described. Strangely it looked like he had been talking when the picture was taken.

The record revealed that Little Dicky was one busy toad, a small time hustler who seemed to make his living working the streets. One would naturally have to conclude that Purvis' preoccupation was pimping. He was arrested at least eight times trying to peddle the flesh of $20.00 hookers, women who should have aged out of the service years ago. In addition he had been arrested four times for lewd behavior involving women, three times for drunk and disorderly conduct, and one time each for assault and for defrauding an innkeeper. Jack estimated that the total jail time he served was sixteen months.

The assault occurred in an emergency room of a hospital. Seems Dicky had had a little too much to drink and was feeling frisky. He required medical care after receiving a beating from a huge bouncer who saw the little guy grab ass a waitress, who just happened to be his wife. For some reason, Purvis was dissatisfied with his care and tried to take it out on a nurse.

The description of this particular incident had made Jack and Loomis guffaw out loud like teens watching the JACKASS crew bust their cup cakes trying ridiculously dangerous stunts. It seemed that Florence Nightingale had taken umbrage with her nasty, little patient and kicked his ass all over again in the emergency room. When the cops arrived, Purvis became belligerent with them. The boys in blue had ended his fun with nightsticks. Then they shackled his bad self and dragged him out of the hospital, feet first.

Later, Jack and Loomis met with their boss and went over what they had. Lieutenant Steve Orlando agreed that they surely had to talk to this clown. Dicky was probably the last person who had seen Milly McCanless alive.

Luckily they found Purvis at home. He lived in a rattrap of a one-bedroom apartment in a ruined duplex that probably should have been condemned as unfit for human occupation.

He answered their knocks barefoot, wearing only a tight pair of tidy whites, growling and hissing like a Tasmanian Devil.

"What the Hell do you want?" he barked, his hairy man-boobs bouncing as he spoke.

When he found out the two men on his doorstep were cops, he upped the ante. He stepped out of his hovel and confronted them with a vengeance.

"Listen you donut chompin' sons of bitches, get off my property. I don't want to buy no Goddamn tickets to the Policemen's Ball. That shit was all a scam for old ladies what got no sense. You pricks GOT no balls. It's good you walk around with those little tin badges what come out of cereal boxes and sport those stun guns and pistols or folks would kick your sorry asses regular. Just climb back into your circus clown car and go see your mommies before I open a can a whip ass. Looks to me like you already had your share," he said, literally pointing to Loomis's face.

Jack seized an opening as Little Dicky caught his breath "Mr. Dicky, we need to ask you a few questions," he said.

"I aint got nothing to say to you pricks. I wouldn't give you the sweat off my balls. And you, you big shit," he said looking straight at Loomis, "you better get your preppy little partner out of my face or I'm going to make him as ugly as you are. Your got so much ugly on you, you could package the stuff and sell it. I'm wondering why the doctor didn't toss your sorry fat ass in the shit can as soon as he laid eyes on your ugly mug. Your Mama must have been total blind cause no woman in her right mind would let a creature like you suck on her tits. Talk about the Devil's spawn...."

Loomis never said a word. He found a bare foot with his shoe and stomped down as hard as he could, putting all his weight into it.

"Mother of Gahhd," screamed Purvis, his beady eyes now open as wide as they could get.

"Oh, I'm so sorry," Loomis said in his most humble baritone voice.

"Please excuse me. I am a little clumsy some times," he added softlly.

Apparently Purvis didn't hear Loomis apologize. As he skipped about, looking every bit like he was playing a game of hopscotch, he continued to threaten and curse. Then he made a slight mistake and made a nasty remark about Loomis' mother and an orangutan.

Loomis said nothing in response. Suddenly he too started hopping around in place alternating feet like an Indian doing a dance, humming a rhythmic melody locals would recognize as the Florida State University's fight song, Then he began to dance in a circle around Purvis, who was still hopping himself, but in place on the one uninjured foot. The Mutt and Jeff pairing looked like they were performing some kind of a weird circus act. Jack, the only one in the audience, had seen this performance before and was enjoying it all over again like watching the Harlem Globetrotters a second time.

Loomis' strange behavior confused and worried the little man. As the big fellow made another pass close by him, Purvis Dicky stopped hopping to keep an eye on him. In so doing he gingerly put his injured foot down to steady himself. He figured that Loomis might try to sucker punch him. Immediately, Loomis lunged at him and hopped right back on that same foot. This time Purvis spun out hopping erratically and then spiraled to the ground with huge tears in his eyes, screaming like a sissy, little boy who had just skinned a knee.

Unfortunately the little hoodlum managed to fall right smack into a fire ant nest that was partially hidden under overgrown shrubbery by the door. Hundreds of the little insects poured out of their home in a fury. Before Little Dicky could think straight they were on him in great numbers, each biting him, seemingly at the very same instant. Purvis screamed again and rolled, and rolled, like a man afire, which in a way he was.

He rolled straight across the yard, off the curb, and into the street. For a second Jack and Loomis froze. They damn well didn't want their suspect to get hit by a car! Quickly they both sprinted out to retrieve him. But, it was too late. A man on a motorcycle roared down the street just as Purvis rolled to a stop in his path. In an instant the biker dropped his machine and slid with it to a grinding halt inches from the speed bump in the road that was Purvis Dicky.

"You dumb asshole," the biker hollered, jumping to his feet. "You tore up my bike you little sonbitch!"

And with that he snatched Purvis off the ground and whacked him hard in the face with an open hand, and then again, back and forth like he was trying to awaken a dead man. Purvis' little eyes began to blink with every blow. His mouth gaped open forming a perfect oval almost like a child watching a fireworks show. Between the blows, he looked out on the world with great fascination and wonder. Oh, he wondered all right. He wondered if he was going to die.

The good guys came to his rescue. They flashed badges and told the biker to back off or go to jail for assault. He readily complied by freeing Purvis and letting him fall hard like a sack of potatoes back on the street. Purvis landed face down, spread eagled with his arms flung out like he was embracing the concrete. The biker, still fuming under his breath, turned, picked up his motorcycle, examined it carefully, and fired it up. He backed the machine off a few yards. Then he accelerated and sped off, riding directly over one of Purvis' out stretched hands.

Jack and Loomis exchanged glances as if to ask if the other had seen that. Then they both cracked up, although Jack was beginning to worry about how to explain broken bones. They helped Little Dicky to his feet and examined him. His hand and foot seemed to function properly and apparently he remained in one piece. But, he was covered in ant bites and banged up like an old Buick in a Demolition Derby.

Loomis wanted to cuff their culprit and throw him into the trunk of the car. But Jack reminded him that they didn't have enough to arrest him. They conferred privately for a second and then returned to Purvis, who had flopped down by the curb.

"Mr. Dicky," Loomis said in his nicest tone of voice, even though the very effort to talk with Purvis Dickey thoroughly pissed him off. "You need to come with us. We need to talk with you at the station."

"What?" Purvis asked, slurring the word like he was drunk.

"Come with us to the station!" Loomis insisted.

"All right," the little fellow responded still shaky and not quite sure where he was.

"Good," said Loomis, in a cheerful way. "We will take good care of you," he said looking straight at Jack with a deadly sarcastic smile.

Before they left they took a look into the blue Impala. They wanted to be able to collaborate the babysitter's testimony including the fact that Purvis had driven her from the bar to her home. Hopefully with the medical examiner's help, they could give evidence in trial to indicate that the victim died shortly thereafter. They would need to secure search warrants to check the car and the apartment in hopes of bagging the murder weapon.

On the way to the jailhouse, Purvis recovered a bit, and soon found his stride.

"You pricks are gonna pay for this," he squawked. And once in gear he just kept at it.

Jack and Loomis sitting up front could do nothing to stop the steady flow of threats and curses short of pulling over, dragging him out of the car, and shooting him. Loomis actually considered doing just that. But, all they could do, was smile and listen to the harangue, admiring the phasing and the off color imagery it created.

Without additional comment they chauffeured Little Dicky to the jailhouse. After borrowing an orange jump suit to cover his nasty little body, they asked the nurse on duty to see to his many ant bites, bruises, and scratches. Purvis behaved himself with this nurse, although he could not stop flirting with her. A grandmother of six, she played along at first until she realized that the creep was serious. In truth he was genuinely pleased to get some attention, particularly from someone other than bikers and cops. Plus, he was truly suffering from those ant bites!

"Gads," she said. "How did you get so messed up?" Then before he could answer, she turned to Jack with, "I bet he tried to escape, didn't he?"

"You could say that," Jack said.

"Escape? Escape?" Dicky hollered. "These bastards jumped me and beat me to a pulp. I am going to sue the Sheriff and close down the whole operation. You wouldn't believe what is going on out in the streets. They violated my constitution. They violated my rights of lib-tee and I want to see a lawyer right..."

Loomis appeared out of nowhere, leaned down and twisted one of Purvis's ears into a cauliflower. Then he ever so quietly whispered directly into Little Dicky's face, "shut up!" And for a time he did.

"We don't want to book him right now. Just patch him up. We'll wait," Loomis added, directing his comments sweetly to the nurse.

Later, Jack and Loomis ushered Purvis into an interview room.

"Thank you for coming down, Mr. Dicky," Loomis said most pleasantly. "We just need to ask you a few questions about Milly McCanless. You have the right to remain silent. You don't have to talk to..."

"Listen you big prick," Dicky said, stopping the cop in mid sentence. "I know my rights. I'm not afraid to talk to your badass cause I didn't do nothing. 'Sides, my lawyers will be seeing the Sheriff in the morning about police brutaltee. You can't get away with what you done. You suckered stomped me. Bet you're scared to step outside with me man to man right now cause I'd wipe the parking lot clean with your sorry butt, and you know it."

"Thank you for your cooperation," Loomis slurred.

Jack decided that he had better intervene. He started off with a few questions concerning Purvis' relationship to the victim. Dicky, turning his back to Loomis, responded pleasantly to Officer Mulkey. He readily admitted knowing her and enjoying her sexual favors a few times, pausing to describe himself as God's gift to women. Next, Jack asked the little man when he had seen her last. Purvis said he wasn't sure. Jack pushed a little and got him to say it could have been early last week.

So it went for a while. Purvis managed to keep his cool and answer the questions directly without acting out. Along the way of course Purvis did not help himself. He talked too much. So when Jack finally told him the woman had been murdered and witnesses put him at the scene, he almost lost it. When he was asked if he knew anything about a baby, with the implication that he may have kidnapped her, he went berserk.

Spittle flew from his mouth as he ranted and raved in protest. After almost exhausting himself unloading on the detectives, he managed to cross over that proverbial line again. He accused the two cops of practicing buggery.

Loomis rose slowly out his chair. Purvis, recognizing immediately that he may have stepped on his own crank, quickly drew his feet up under himself and sat Indian style, eyes wide open expecting the worst. But, Loomis simply walked out of the interview room and returned with a cup of coffee. He asked Purvis if he wanted some. Getting a little parched from his diatribe, the little man readily accepted the offer. But he could not leave it at that. He had to minimize Loomis like he was a waiter at his service.

Loomis walked over in front of Purvis with the steaming cup. Blocking the camera that was taping the interview with his bulk, Loomis surreptitiously poured the contents into Mr. Dicky's lap, walked back to his chair and sat down.

It was not the boiling hot coffee that got McDonalds in trouble but Mr. Dicky did feel an unusual burning sensation between his thighs. He squirmed as the coffee soaked through the jumpsuit and into his filthy drawers, gave the cops a pathetic look, shut his yap, and made a mental note not to ever screw with the big guy again.

After about an hour, the officers had nothing. Purvis proudly admitted being with Milly. He insisted that she was alive when he left, and the baby was asleep in her crib. He challenged the officers in a very nice and respectful tone to prove otherwise. Then he let his mouth get him into serious trouble

Purvis with great bravado offered to take a polygraph test and told them they could search his house and his car all they wanted. He said over and over again that he had nothing to hide and was as innocent as the day is long. Jack got him to make a written statement including all of that, thanked him again, and asked him to wait for a while. They would be back. Of course they did not tell Little Dicky that it might be a few hours.

Then the two cops plus Nannette, the crime scene investigator, headed straight back to Dicky's place, immediately taking him up on his permission to let them search his house and car. They gloved up and started with the Impala because the apartment smelled like the carcass of a dead turkey. After flipping through old fast food cups and containers, candy wrappers, porn magazines, and used condoms in the interior, they opened the trunk. Jack and Loomis gingerly tossed the contents a little. It was Loomis who spotted it first.

"Can you believe this?" Loomis asked excitedly.

"Wow!" said Jack spotting the bloody freezer bag immediately.

Both stepped back, each one grinning like little boys who had just found a sack of coins.

"We got that sucker!" Loomis said proudly as Nannette moved in to take pictures and put the knife into evidence.

"Holy Mackerel!" said Jack almost giddy with delight.

"You and me partner!" shouted Loomis playfully. "We just nailed that little sucker."

They continued to celebrate as Nannette quietly went about her work. She was happy for them. It was rare that finding what appeared to be the murder weapon was ever so easy.

Searching the house produced little of interest although Nannette did take more pictures and bagged a few more items that might prove helpful later. All three marveled at the number of porn pictures and magazines they found in his bedroom. They decided to bag only a sample of the material because the collection looked like fairly tame stuff with no hint of sexual sadism and violence.

Their initial conclusion that Mr. Dicky was their man started to unravel a bit on the way back to the station. They really didn't know how to account for the missing child, and they were not comfortable without a readily apparent motive. There was more.

"Mulk, why does little Purvis knife the gal that lets him slither into her bed?" asked Loomis. "Even if he paid her some, she took that nasty creep home, for crying out loud. Who'd call that living if no gal would give in to no man what's ugly as sin? Seems the twerp ought to have been eternally grateful to her. Then cut her like that? That's cruel, man!"

"I hear you partner," said Jack in reply. "But the evidence sure points his way. He was the last person to see that woman alive. And we bagged what looks like the murder weapon. Let's just take what we have, go back and see what the lieutenant thinks."

Nannette did not promise to have DNA results any time soon, so they freed Purvis when they returned but said nothing about the knife. They figured he was not going anywhere. Then they conferred with Lieutenant Orlando. They decided to file for an arrest warrant anyway. The knife itself coupled with the baby sitter's testimony and the rest of the evidence they had was enough to establish probable cause. The next afternoon after securing the warrant they picked up Purvis again.

Within hours of dropping the capital murder bomb on his ugly, bald dome and leaving him hissing and pissing in his cell, like a furious caged raccoon, Jack, but not Loomis, began to get urgent messages from him. They came from far and wide. Purvis proclaimed his innocence at the top of his lungs, as only he knew how.

Chapter 15

It was not until late that afternoon that Dave Boyette, the cop who had discovered an abandoned baby in Atmore, Alabama, learned about the murder. A fellow officer had viewed a news report on Channel 3 on line. The website carried a fairly detailed account of the crime, including a reference that a child may have been taken from the home of the deceased.

That tidbit of information hit officer Boyette right between the eyes. Finding the baby had almost been a religious experience for Dave. Unmarried and in his mid thirties he had simply been walking through his life. He took each day as it came, cashed it in, and waited for the next. In truth he hung around the small police station a great deal because he really had little else to do.

But, that changed that night as a baby came into his life. He found energy and purpose in saving her. He was openly optimistic about the future of the little one. He imagined that a desperate young mother with no options for her child did her best to find a safe place for the little girl and managed to get her into the hands of people who would love and care for her. He dreamed of uniting the baby with her mother, helping her get to her feet, so that she could in fact raise her child. Beyond that he recklessly allowed himself to imagine adopting the kid, even though he knew he would be a very unlikely candidate.

He immediately phoned a buddy who had transferred to the Escambia County Sheriff's Department in Pensacola, Florida. His friend put him on hold for a while. Then suddenly he was patched into Jack Mulkey. After introducing himself and excitedly explaining his connection, he almost begrudgingly asked the key question.

"I guess you guys are looking for a little girl?" he queried.

"You got that right. We are missing a baby wearing something pink, or in a pink blanket."

Dave froze for a second. He now knew for certain that the baby the cops found missing in Pensacola was his baby. He felt odd, almost ill at ease. He wanted to be happy for the little kid but now felt sad, like someone close to him was slipping away. He had visited with the child in her shelter home two or three times a day. When off duty he would sit quietly on a front porch rocker and hold her for hours. He was not sure why he felt so close to her, but the shelter parents had noticed. He had bonded.

"Dave, are you still there," asked Jack after a long pause.

"Yea. Yea, I'm here. I was just thinking, I guess," Dave responded.

"What happens now?" Dave asked.

"I'm assuming your child welfare folks have her in shelter care up there. We need to get the Florida people and your folks together. Be sure to call them, and I'll do the same here. They can sort all this out. You know we think the mother was murdered, right? Anyway, they will probably want to do some DNA testing to make sure. Let's keep this out of the news if we can until the results are in."

Dave was not really listening. He had not actually seen the TV broadcast and had not connected the dots between the murder victim and the little girl. His hopes of finding the young mother were as dead now as the woman they found savagely slain in her bed.

"I'm not sure there's anything else for us," Jack said suddenly, jolting Dave back to the phone call. "We think we have the guy who did it behind bars already. We're not positive, but he looks good for it."

"Yea. That's great," managed Dave.

"Is there a father?" Dave said quickly thereafter, the thought suddenly entering his mind.

"He's not on our radar," Jack said. "Right now, we aren't looking for him either. As I understand it, the agency with legal custody of the child is required to complete a diligent search, you know, a serious attempt to ferret out the parents if possible before the court will even consider freeing it for adoption."

Dave heard that last word loud and clear. Maybe there was a way after all he thought, a broad smile brightening his mood.

Chapter 16

As the workweek began, Jack sat at his desk, quietly thinking as the normal noise of the squad room echoed around him. When he told Dave Boyette that he would contact Children's Services in Florida, he opened a book that had been closed for over three years. He had not considered the normal chain of command. He had not considered that the matter might best be handled by his lieutenant or at least run by him for courtesy. Also, he had not thought at what level in the hierarchy of the children's agency his information would normally be handled. He even knew Ralph Munch, the agency's area supervisor, whom he had met before at meetings when he accompanied the Sheriff. No, he was going to make the call. And he would be calling Beth Jacoby.

He found a vacant office he could use and dialed a central number for the agency. It took a while to get connected to the right location. When Beth suddenly said hello, he nearly froze.

Beth and Jack had grown up together. They lived on the same street, and their parents were close friends. The two families often vacationed together at a small cottage on a lake near Tallahassee. Beth and Jack became close, almost like siblings. Their bemused parents watched them wrestle and romp, swim and dunk each other, and run about like two unruly bear cubs for years. In middle school the sibling relationship began to turn. The two were still close but in a very different way. By high school they were going steady. The adults, parents, teachers, and others who knew them just took for granted that the handsome pair would be married in the near future.

The two jumped that gun a bit. One evening as they worked together on a science project at her house, they found themselves alone. Her parents respected Jack and knew he would not try to get intimate with their daughter. They went to a movie. But they failed to consider that their beautiful little girl had a mind of her own. She encouraged Jack to kiss and fondle her. Ultimately it was she who led him upstairs to her own bedroom. And there beneath the ruffled canopy and the shelves of stuffed animals, she gave herself to him.

The sex actually frightened them both, and they never pulled a stunt like that again. Perhaps it led in some way to the collapse of their destiny as high school sweethearts soon to wed. Like other such close couples, they drifted apart by the end of their senior year.

"Beth," he finally said. "This is Jack. Jack Mulkey."

"Jack? How are you? It sure has been a long time."

"I guess it has," he said bravely, almost like their separation was of no real concern to him. But of course it was.

"I've got some information for your agency, and I thought I'd just call you. I wasn't really sure whom to call. If you could, just relay it on to the party you think should be involved."

"Sure Jack," she said, with a tiny hint of disappointment in her voice.

He explained the situation, and she took notes. She then told him what would probably happen next, and he took notes.

When they had finished the shoptalk, she said rather abruptly, "Well, thank you, Jack, I'll take care of it. Is there anything else?"

Jack was struck by the finality in her tone. She seemed ready to disconnect again. He knew that this brief official sounding call might be the very last exchange between them. It really would not matter if he failed, but he had to try and try right now.

"Beth, Ah, I'd like to see you again. You know, catch up."

"What?" she asked, like she couldn't quite get the meaning of what he had just said.

"Can I coax you into lunch or dinner sometime?" he asked, cool as the bottom side of a pillow but warming with anxiety to say the least.

"I'd love that," she said. "Yes. Let's definitely do that."

"Great!" Jack responded happily. "How about lunch on Wednesday?"

"That sounds great to me," she answered quickly and without hesitation.

They discussed details and sealed the deal. When they both hung up, each felt more alive than they had in a long time.

But later, Beth began to wonder about the wisdom of seeing Jack again. She had acted impulsively without giving it much thought. She began to convince herself that times had changed, that the magic was no longer there, that getting involved with him again now might not be the best thing for her. She loved her work. She didn't know if she really wanted to sacrifice her independence.

But, then again, it was he. It was Jack!

Chapter 17

Later Monday morning Cletus called together his investigators for an impromptu meeting in their so-called conference room while Ernie covered the office and manned the phones.

"I just have an announcement to make," Cletus said. "Let me see how good the scuttlebutt is around here. What am I going to say?"

"I heard we would not be able to fill that vacant investigator position," said Vicky Snow.

"Damn! I thought you might not know this," said Cletus. "OK," he added, singling to the group that Vicky was spot on. "I just received a call this morning form Ralph Munch. The vacant position will be frozen indefinitely. There is no budget for it. It will no doubt remain frozen until the beginning of the new budget cycle in July."

"The Pharaoh demands that we make bricks with no straw?" cracked Bill.

"Unfortunately there is more," continued Cletus. "The Clerk Typist position has been cut from the budget. It is gone. The rationale is simple. A legislative budget committee discovered that the agency was carrying almost one hundred positions that had been vacant for over a year. They concluded that we didn't need them and simply cut them out of the budget permanently. They never asked. They just did it, and they refused to reinstate them even when they were told that the agency had to keep positions open to meet the salary budget."

"Damn," said Bill, echoing the sentiments of the entire group.

"What kind of reverse logic is that? Won't we have to freeze even more positions in the future?" Bill went on.

"There was some talk that they would increase the salary dollars for us. We will just have to wait and see," Cletus replied.

"Look," said Cletus. "I'm sorry about this but that's the way it is. As far as I know there will be no cuts in the expense budget so you will continue to get reimbursed for travel," he said jokingly. Then he added," I guess the state is not broke yet."

Cletus was proud of his staff. They were all dedicated employees. It really had very little to do with him although he did hire most of them. It was something they brought to the job. They cared. They took their responsibility to children very seriously. He knew before he opened his mouth that they would keep doing the best they could. But silently he wondered why the protection of innocent kids never made the list of absolute priorities. Sadly, he doubted that it ever would.

"Anyone else got anything to say?" Cletus asked.

"Yes," said Vicky. "Bill, what's happening on that starvation case?"

"By court order, the little girl is temporarily living with her grandmother in Marianna. The mother is already seeing Larry Booker at least once a week. She was very cooperative about that, and I'm sure she will continue with the mental health counseling. She bought into the roommate's psychosis. The old gal is truly delusional. She convinced the mother that her child was possessed by demons that could only be controlled by limiting the little girl's food intake. The diagnosis, which I never heard of before, is Shared Psychotic Disorder. The mother has already dumped the roommate, the first step in recovery. Further, she is never to be in contact with her again. If the judge agrees, that provision and the counseling will be court ordered conditions for reunification. We will seek a protective services order for a period of long term supervision just to be sure, but it really does look like she will be fine."

"I've got some news," Beth announced, changing the subject. "I have already told Cletus. Do any of you remember Milly McCanless? She was murdered last week, Friday, I believe. Anyway, they have found the missing baby in Alabama. She's in shelter care up there. They don't want to break the story until they get DNA results but it seems certain. Who worked that case? Was it you Bill?"

"Not me. That name sounds familiar though," Bill said.

"Eleanor, was it you?" asked Beth trying again.

"Yes, I completed an investigation involving her a long time ago," Eleanor replied quickly. An infant died accidentally in her care. If I recall correctly, she fell asleep on a couch with a baby and subsequently suffocated the poor child by rolling over on it. She was intoxicated at the time, and the house was a filthy mess. The court here removed her two other children. They are growing up in foster care but there is hope they may still find adoptive parents for them soon."

"She must have had another baby," Eleanor said, shaking her head sadly. "For a relatively small town we do get a full share of human misery."

That kicked off a few minutes of chatter concerning murder and intrigue. Cletus let it spill out for a while and then got the group to move on. Bill opened by asking a question of his own.

"Have you seen or heard anything more from Leonard Samford?"

"Who?" asked Eleanor.

"That charming fellow that threatened Shanice and Cletus," Bill offered.

"I haven't seen hide nor hair of that man since he barged in here last week," said Cletus. "What about the case, Shanice?" he asked.

"I found out the family had been involved with child welfare folks in Alabama several times. They are sending me the records. The dependency hearing is scheduled in a couple of weeks. I can't see any way the kids will be going back home. Of course he has to face domestic violence charges in criminal court as well. I'll tell you guys one thing, I still worry about that freak. I don't think he has forgotten about us. But, what can you do?"

Shanice left it at that, and Cletus said nothing. He knew what to do, and he had already done it.

"Anything else for the good of the order," said Cletus, with a slight smile masking his real thoughts about Leonard Samford.

"Yes," said Vicky. "Did anyone bring donuts?"

That effectively ended the impromptu meeting. The entire group, including Cletus Jones, seized advantage of the assemblage and took some time to enjoy each other's company.

"Hey, Mr. Bill, how did you get that bruise on your forehead?" asked Beth

"You don't want to know," Bill answered, effectively making sure that everyone there most certainly did.

"Come on, Bill," said Shanice. What have you been up to?"

"Well," Bill started, "I went out to do a little counseling on Saturday with a woman I met on the job not too long ago. I had worked a false report before involving her, and I guess she took a liking to me. She called for me through the Abuse Registry, and I visited with her for a while. That's it," he concluded.

"So this gal gave you a bruise?" pressed Vicky.

"On my forehead, on my butt, and to my ego to boot," said Bill, grinning from ear to ear.

So he told his story, told on himself. The entire group roared with laughter as he dished out details a small serving at a time. They became so loud that Ernie and a worker from down the hall came to investigate. So Bill recapped a little and then added the finish.

As the meeting broke up and the staff drifted toward their own offices, Ernie grabbed Bill for some of the details he had missed. When Bill had answered all his questions, Ernie said, "My life is so dull in comparison."

"Come on, Ernie," said Bill. "You aren't fooling me. I know you get out and have some fun once in a while. I recall the time you showed up at a party dressed as a woman accompanied by a beautiful woman dressed as a man. Remember that?"

"I sure do," answered Ernie shyly with a twinkle in his eyes.

"Well, as a matter of fact I'm going to a play tonight with an old friend," offered Ernie with a smile.

"Now what did I just say? What play are you going to see?" asked Bill.

"A student presentation at the University of West Florida," answered Ernie. "It should be fun."

Chapter 18

Ernie met Marcus, a friend, that evening at the latter's apartment soon after 6:15 P.M. The play they were going to see started at 8:30 P.M. He hadn't seen his old friend in almost a year. Never a love interest, Marcus Velney had just shown up in Ernie's life, a troubled man who from the very beginning didn't quite know who he was.

"Wow," Ernie said flatly walking in the door as he took in his friend's new décor.

"It sure is different, Marcus. I have to be totally honest with you though. I miss the old look. What did you do with all the glass sculptures? Your place is so unlike you. It's utilitarian and you have all you need, but..."

"It's not me? Is that what you mean?" asked Marcus.

Ernie didn't answer at first. He politely waited until Marcus asked him to sit down. Once comfortably ensconced in an armchair, Marcus followed up with a tray of crackers and an artichoke dip.

Marcus was a lumpy fellow, short, and partially bald with a chubby cherub-like face. He supported a substantial toneless body with oversized, flabby legs. He greeted his old friend in designer sweat clothes that could have indicated he had been working out. But obviously he had not. Marcus was soft more so than obese. The extra flesh and the hair loss made him look older than he actually was. Ernie knew him to be thirty-five. He was considered handsome once, but he had managed to lose the strong raw boned, masculine look he once sported. The defining lines were now hidden under an overall puffiness like someone bloated by too much booze. Ernie was saddened at the obvious way his buddy had let himself go. He wondered to himself if Marcus were drinking again.

After a few bites of food, Ernie continued the conversation.

"Well, since you asked what I meant by my rather insensitive remarks, I have been wondering how you have been doing since you got back from Texas. How did that go?"

"Ernie, I'm not going to say that overcoming is possible for everyone, but I have put my former lifestyle behind me a long time ago, soon after I told you that I would. The week in Texas was a wonderful experience. It strengthened me anew. I am a changed man, and I am happy," Marcus stated proudly.

"Well, I'm so glad you are happy, Marcus. That's really the important thing, isn't it?" Ernie responded.

"Yes. And what about you, Ernie? Can you honestly say you are happy?"

"I've never been unhappy, I guess. I'm alive and well in my own skin," Ernie replied a little nervously.

"But, you can change," Marcus persisted. "All you have to do is to place your faith in God. We were not created with a longing for members of the same sex. But, as sensual beings we all are tempted to pursue sexual encounters, some with men, some with women, some with both. Satan is persistent. We must resist temptations. The same goes for heterosexuals. Think of Bill Clinton and that guy who ran for President while cheating on his wife? Lord, think of the mess we all make of our lives because we choose to let our eyes wander over the wrong partners," Marcus went on.

Ernie had seen both men and women struggle with their sexuality. It was always painful for him. He had been lucky. His parents never said a word until one day he simply asked his father about it. His father never blinked. If his parents were sad or disappointed, he never knew of it. They seemed to know exactly what to do and say, as if they had a manual with instructions to guide them. They never once gave in to doubt or fear and they never let him wallow in it either. Despite being socially abhorrent to many, Ernie learned that self-confidence and a smile won him a place in the world, exactly as he had been born into it.

"Look Marcus," said Ernie. "I don't want to debate this with you. I'm so happy for you. I'm proud of you too. But I am who I am. I don't know anything different. I guess I'm like most people. I was born with certain characteristics, and I grew up. I never worried about being someone who I shouldn't be. I have never once considered changing. Let's drop this subject. We never get anywhere arguing, do we?"

"All right," Marcus said. "We'll drop it. But I really wish you would go to Texas with me some time."

"Oh gosh," Ernie replied sadly. "I really don't like the fact that many people judge and despise me just for who I am. But. Oh, I'm sorry Marcus, I really will change the subject."

They made small talk for a while discussing trouble at city hall. Then Ernie hit upon a subject that changed the whole tenor of the evening.

"What did you think of the Rogers-Smithson affair? You used to work for him, didn't you?"

Marcus did not answer at first. His eyes widened, and he swelled up in his chair His face flushed in crimson. A slight tic appeared on one cheek.

"That bastard!" snapped Marcus, immediately aggressive and angry. He followed with a frothy mouthed tirade that shocked and frightened Ernie. The rant made him push back deeper into the cushions of his chair, literally shrinking from the violence in Marcus' voice.

He was the one that found out I was dating other men. He tormented me in the worst way. He encouraged the others too, and they were all too happy to oblige. I became a target for every abuse they could muster. I had been his best salesman hands down. But after he exposed me he made it impossible for me to make a living there. I had to quit to survive financially. I have never really recovered either."

"He raped that little girl sure as shooting. That creep was a sexual predator in the worse way. He always went after younger men, well boys really. He hurt them too. I just assume that poor girl had not filled out. She probably looked like a boy at the time. Oh, I hate that SOB. I'd kill that prick if I had a chance."

"Marcus!" Ernie gasped.

"My word! I had no idea. Please..."

"Oh, drop that façade, Ernie," Marcus said loudly. "Don't forget my dear old pal, you weren't always wrapped so tight either. I remember a time you were carrying a switchblade!"

"I just thought about that. It would have been for protection and you know it. I would never dream of trying to hurt anyone," Ernie protested.

"You have no idea what he did to me. You ask about how I'm doing? Well, do you really want to know? Do you?" Marcus demanded, ignoring Ernie's lie about the knife.

"Just sit there with your sanctimonious little smile on your face while I tell you exactly how I'm doing. I'm for shit! I'm miserable and suicidal. I see a therapist every week. I take two different powerful antidepressants, and I drink like a fish! How's that my friend!" Marcus bellowed, still brimming with anger.

Ernie was shocked into silence. In truth he did not know what to do or say. He knew that Marcus was trying very hard to come to grips with his sexuality. But this was different. Marcus' explosion was primitive, boiling out of a cauldron that had been simmering for years. It was all about Rogers-Smithson and yet had nothing to do with him at all.

Ernie understood that since the very first time one man looked outside his tribe at another man, sensing something alien, something to be feared, violence erupted and the world knew hate. He and Marcus were different than most others. And they were often despised because of it. Perhaps, to his own peril, Marcus chose to deny himself. He had heard the cock crow many times. He had wanted to be accepted, to find peace. But in self-denial peace now totally eluded him.

"Marcus," Ernie dared. "That evil man is not what this is all about. Maybe you and I should forget the play at UWF and just talk."

"Yes," Marcus managed to say, still heavily breathing the air of discontent.

Chapter 19

Later that same Monday evening Beth, who was on-call, received the report that all investigators dread. A child was dead under suspicious circumstances. It would be coded for possible neglect. An immediate response was required. Beth took down the pertinent information, changed out of her shorts and top for something more appropriate, and rode the Mustang though the night.

This was a first for her. Beth had talked with her veteran coworker, Eleanor Porter, about a death case she had handled several years ago. A drunken boy friend had flown into a rage because a baby would not stop crying. The little girl, no more than six months old, had been thrown hard to the floor and silenced forever. A quiet conversation with Eleanor, who said she never got over that case, was the extent of Beth's experience. She hoped that she would be strong enough to deal with what she must face, walking in the door.

She arrived in time to see the baby. The body was about to be loaded into the removal service van. She approached the still open cargo doors, flashed her ID, and accepted a silent offer to examine the child. A cover that hid the child was pushed aside. The image of the baby in a pale death mask became permanently etched into her mind's eye. She would wake up in a sweat often thereafter in the middle of the night haunted by what she had just seen.

Beth only glanced at the lifeless toddler. Holding her eyes upon it would have been more than she could bear. Even so, she felt her blood run cold. Shivers ran up her spine and a gut- wrenching churn began to rumble in the pit of her stomach. She tried to regain composure, to ask the attendant an intelligent question or two, but her voice would not come. Instead she choked on her words, making a sound like someone gagging down a bit of bad food.

"Are you OK?" asked the man softly.

"I'll be fine," she managed, still sounding like there was something caught in her throat.

"How do you ever get used to this?" Beth asked.

"Funny," he answered. "I was just about to ask you the same thing."

Beth eased herself away but stumbled a little. She had to rest a hand on the massive trunk of an old oak tree to steady herself. For a moment or two she just stood there in the shadows. She tried valiantly to gather her wits. Remembering her role in this kind of situation, she steeled herself to meet the Mom who will now live forever with the death of her own child hanging about her neck like the heaviest of millstones.

She walked with purpose then straight to the front door and entered without a knock. She bumped right into a tough looking police officer sporting a lieutenant's badge holding a toddler, and Ed Kambler, a medical examiner investigator. They were both glad to see her. Apparently they had been waiting for someone to arrive from Children's Services because they could not just leave the mother of the dead child alone.

"Hi. I'm Steve Orlando from the Sheriff's Department. You're the investigator from the Department of Children's Services, aren't you? I think we met once or twice before," the police officer said warmly.

"Yes," she responded, reminding him of her name and showing him her ID.

"Great! I need to get going. My arm is killing me," he said jostling the child a little to prove the point. "I still don't understand how women can cart a kid around for hours and think nothing of it. I just thought the little guy needed a little love. We have no reason to suspect foul play, and I am supposed to be at another call. I hope you don't mind, but can I turn him over to you now?"

"Why yes," she said, taking the boy who did not seem to mind although he eyed her closely during the transfer.

"Go ahead, Steve," said Ed. "I'll fill Beth in on a few things."

In the few moments it took for the officer to leave, Beth caught a glimpse of a lifeless form on a couch. Ed noticing, asked her to step outside. Still carrying the toddler on her hip, Beth followed him out the door.

Once out in the night air again the medical investigator started right in. "The mother's name is Barbara Copton. I think she said she was twenty-two. The young lady is a basket-case as you would expect. She may be in shock. Keep an eye on her. I think her husband is overseas serving in the Navy. She wasn't exactly clear about any of this. But, you will need to contact them. They will get the husband back here as quickly as they can. In the meantime she will need someone to stay with her. I don't think there are any relatives close by."

"All that we were able to learn from her is that she was bathing the baby girl, who just turned two, when this little three-year old started screaming in the living room. She ran to check on him and left the little one alone in the tub. When she got back the child was face down in the water. When I got here the water was still in the tub. I measured it at four inches deep at the center of the tub. Apparently the mother yanked her daughter out and tried giving her mouth to mouth. She was literally coming apart on the 911 call, and it took the operator some time to get an address."

"But here's the thing. She told me her son had been bitten by their dog. It's one of those hyper little terriers. I put him in the garage. Bottom line, I didn't find a mark on that boy. The shallow depth of the water bothers me too, but a little one can drown in less. I honestly believe it was an accident, but for now I'm leaving it open. I need to examine the body at the lab. Also I very much want the results of your investigation. After you have completed your work, please contact me as soon as possible."

Beth could not get past an image that flashed through her head, an image of a small girl on an autopsy table. She felt nauseous again like something alive was slowly crawling in her stomach.

"OK," she said blankly, feeling like she had been told very important information by a teacher in school but had already forgotten what it was.

"Do you have any questions?" he asked.

"The dog is in the garage?" she mumbled, struggling to understand the details she had been given while still contemplating the enormity of a baby's tragic death. She regretted her response immediately. She guessed he probably wondered about her as he just stared at her quizzically and did not answer. "I mean, how is the mother doing? Will I be able to talk to her?"

"I sure hope so," he advised. "Listen, Miss Jacoby, I really want your professional opinion regarding the possibility of neglect. Please call me in the morning."

"I'll do it," she replied, the word "professional" suddenly reminding her of her responsibility and renewing some of the confidence that had before she was staggered with the sight of the dead baby.

"Well, I'll leave it with you then. So it's all yours. Are you all right with that?" he asked.

"I'll be fine," she said, perhaps too casually.

She watched the investigator briefly as he climbed into his car and drove off. The removal service van had already left. It was her thing now, she thought. Let's go girl she said to herself, trying to ready herself as best she could be for what lay ahead.

She found Barbara Copton, the young girl and mother of the deceased, sitting like a rag doll on a couch. Her back was bowed and her head partially down, her eyes focused on nothing along the floorboard on the opposite side of the room. Her arms were linked at the wrists as if indivisible straps bound them. Her knees met but her feet were splayed awkwardly. If Beth had not known otherwise, she could have assumed that the mother had been punched hard in the stomach. In a way she had.

The boy leaned down a little and pointed to a Teddy Bear dressed like a sailor on the floor. Gingerly she set him on his little feet, and he promptly trotted to the bear, grabbed it to his chest, and sat on the floor. The boy told the bear in a parental tone that it was time for a bath. He paused for a moment and held the bear up to his face. Then the bear told him in no uncertain terms that he didn't want to. A smattering of song followed. The bear danced. Beth couldn't tell who was singing, the child or the bear.

It finally sunk in that there was no one else around. Surely Barbara had at least one friend. For it was hard for adults to talk to bears. Wow, Beth thought. How could this young woman cope with this alone?

Beth stood quietly for a moment then took a deep breath. Next, she introduced herself. She was amazed that she even bothered to mouth her standard spiel about the agency receiving a report and so forth. Her words seemed to echo as if spoken in an empty room. But it was Barbara Copton who was vacant.

Beth now realized that she had to be the friend.

Silently Beth slipped on to the couch beside the young woman, who actually looked like a child herself. She was twenty-two but looked eighteen or nineteen if that, thin and pale, with stringy ash blonde hair. She smelled of vomit and Beth noticed stains on her T shirt. It was obvious that she was totally lost to the events of the evening. The girl continued to stare off into space and never acknowledged that another person had joined her. Beth was about to begin a soothing monologue when she thought better of it. She simply moved closer and pulled the young mother into her arms.

The bereaved woman allowed herself to be cradled. She snuggled closer in Beth's embrace. Then she started to cry. It was soft at first. She trembled and sobbed quietly pouring out single, large tears like the first drops of a spring rain. Soon, however, she began to spasm with great fits of anguish, tears now flowing in torrents. Beth held on but let her go. There seemed to be no end to her torment as her whole body wracked rhythmically in the pain of desperate loss. The grief intensified, and the girl now groaned almost like she was in the throes of passion. Deeper and deeper into the abyss she fell until finally she could no longer physically sustain the torture. Almost as quickly as it had begun, her crying ceased and her body relaxed.

The boy had pulled back against the wall in terror. He clung to the bear desperately, wide eyed and close to panic. Beth called to him cheerfully. She explained that his mother needed to cry just like he did when he was upset. It was good to cry she explained. Then she invited the lad to join them on the couch. She repeated several times that his mother was going to be fine. As she said it, she wondered if that was a lie.

The boy calmed a bit and stared at her listening intently. Somehow his mother made eye contact with him and offered him a weak smile through eyes still brimming with the last of her tears. He rose slowly and waddled over to the couch dragging the Teddy by one arm behind him. He stood by his mother's knees, reached out and patted her on her leg. Soon Beth was able to ease the little boy up to sit beside her, placing herself in the middle, one arm for each. He leaned forward looking at the two women carefully and then nestled down with Sailor Bear, his tiny thumb finding his mouth.

Beth held on to both of them for a while. The boy fell asleep at her hip. She didn't quite know what else to do at the moment so she just sat there on that couch. It certainly felt right. She guessed that if the roles were reversed she would want someone to hold on to her too.

Time drifted by. Beth shut her eyes and listened to her heartbeat. Then she felt the young woman stir.

"I'm here for you," Beth said, with words that surprised her. It was almost like another person in the room had spoken. As no one else was there, she acknowledged the phase as coming from somewhere deep inside her where humans are wired for compassion. It was not something she would normally say, but here and now, holding on to a wounded soul, she meant every word of it.

Still silent, Barbara Copton lifted her head to face the stranger who had just spoken to her.

"I'm sorry about your top," she said quietly, referring to the dark spot on Beth's blue blouse.

"Don't worry about it," replied Beth softly. "Tears don't leave a stain."

And so the two women spoke for the first time. Beth tried to keep it going but in truth they managed little real communication. Beth started poorly. She introduced herself and tried to explain why she was there. That declaration prompted the first of many new fits of tears. Beth wanted to move on. Unfortunately there were no tomorrows for the young girl. Barbara Copton was very close to being totally consumed with the loss of her baby. She was paralyzed by it. It had coiled around her like a huge snake and was now squeezing the life out of her. The girl could barely manage to breathe, think or do anything else but allow herself to suffer. She was standing very close to the edge.

Beth became a little frantic herself. What on earth was she doing here? She knew how to deal with people who lost loved ones but had no experience with those who may have caused their death. She was no psychologist. But down deep Beth knew that Barbara's guilt, if left unchecked, would eventually push her over the edge and kill her.

Ironically Beth could not yet tell the young woman that she had no reason to feel guilty. For all that she knew the girl might have somehow been negligent. But, Lord, it sure didn't seem that way at all.

She too now took on some of the anguish that Eleanor had once described. What to do next? The simple opportunity to comfort the devastated mother was much preferred to the role of a pseudo cop attempting to fix responsibility for a possible crime. Negligent or not, Beth knew that this girl was standing lost at a crossroad. Somehow she needed to be given directions in order to find her way home.

Beth decided to try to steer Barbara away from the death of the little girl by focusing her attention on her son. In truth the boy probably needed his Mom right now more than ever before. First she tried to help the girl understand that the path that lay ahead would be long and difficult. She would need counseling and a great deal of support.

Then Beth made her point. Barbara's son had lost his sister. He was troubled too. He could not walk down that road without help either. She, Barbara Copton, had to take his hand or carry him.

Perhaps with the realization of the truth in Beth's words, the young mother broke down again. She cried out that she could not do it. She wept once more, but not with the agony of before. She had wept past the point that she could continue to draw those bitter tears. Then slowly she quieted as if she had no more energy for it.

Beth held her close without saying a word. She felt very tired. Stress was attacking her body, robbing it of strength. The muscles in her neck were taut, almost painful. Her back ached and the arm that cradled Barbara Copton tingled for the lack of circulation. But, she was tired in another way too. Like Barbara she had begun to lose her resolve. Her thinking was beginning to cloud over again. "The dog is in the garage," she had asked.

Eleanor Porter had warned her that the death of a child wounded all that came to bear witness, not just the parents. She said that one had to be strong, one had to be tough. As Beth moved her arm a little to supply it with blood, she began to talk to herself. She was the fighter, wasn't she? She had a black belt for crying out loud. Cletus occasionally called her the Kung Fu Fighter. They all thought she was as confident as you could get. And so she was. It was time to get off the damn couch and get going. As her grandfather liked to say, "Let's do something even if it's wrong." So she eased out away from Barbara and stood up and straightened her back.

She reached down and pulled Barbara up too. Standing erect Beth grasped the mother's shoulders and looked directly into her eyes. Then she told her straight up that she was strong because all women were strong. It was probably an exaggeration but it sounded great. She followed up with a litany of things that a wife and mother had to do for their families. She gave examples of the self-sacrifice, courage and strength of women who had faced adversity. She talked about Jacqueline Kennedy, Coretta Scott King and others, forgetting that her student was probably too young to know who they were. It didn't matter though. Barbara Copton seemed to respond.

Face to face Beth continued, as if drawing a picture for Barbara, describing a totally difficult challenge for the whole family with Barbara in the lead, moving herself, her husband and her little boy on past the long shadow of this night. Barbara Copton tried to understand, to comprehend what she had to do, now and tomorrow and the day after that. When the conversation reminded her of the death of her daughter, however, she broke down again. But Beth did not allow

Barbara to languish any longer in the temporary comfort of tears. She kept talking. Pleading. Pulling. Pushing.

Somehow the two made progress. Beth drove home the fact that Barbara would never fully recover from the experience. She would have setbacks. It was natural. But, she also seemed to convince her that with help of others, she could pick herself off the floor and take care of her son and husband.

Eventually Barbara responded to Beth's insistence that she needed someone to stay with her. To Beth amazement, Barbara actually picked up the phone. She was literally able to call a friend and express herself without breaking down. The friend promised to be at the house within the hour. Beth made a mental note to confer with the Navy Wives Association for support later on as well.

Finally Beth convinced the mother to take her son and put him to bed. She knew the grieving mother needed to touch and hold her other child, to lay hands on him, to love him. In preparation for bed, the Mom found a mat, put it on the floor next to the couch and gently placed her son on it in order to change his diaper. As she removed it, Beth remembered what the coroner had said about the absence of a bite mark on the boy. It hit her that the coroner might not have removed the diaper to look for wounds.

She leaned down and closely examined the boy's exposed body. And there it was. On his hip were three slight puncture wounds that barely broke the skin. She asked the mother to hold off for a moment and excused herself to run to the car for her camera. Upon return Barbara rose and Beth kneeled by the sleeping child. She took several pictures of the wounds. As she did so, she carefully explained why the pictures were so vitally important. Then Beth put the camera aside and diapered up the little fellow.

The girl had watched Beth intently with eyes that seemed to widen as the photos were being taken. As Beth closed the last Velcro strap something came over the grieving mother. She faced Beth directly and cried out. "I didn't drown my baby. Please tell me that you believe me."

"Barbara, I want you to listen to me carefully. I believe you. And I will make others believe in you as well. The pictures are important because they represent hard evidence that your boy did in fact scream out in pain. You were distracted like any other mother would be in similar circumstances. It will be extremely difficult for you to ever forget this night. You will never forget your baby. But try, try very hard, to forget any idea that her passing was your fault."

The two women stood looking at each other. Their eyes locked. Right then and there, Barbara actually seemed to pull herself together. She physically stood taller, some color returned to her cheeks. She managed a slight smile, stooped down, and lifted her son into her arms.

Soon the friend arrived. May Frank, who was an older woman, a mother of four teens, and a member of the Navy Wives Association. She advised Beth to contact Navy personnel immediately, explaining that the brass would need to know. She found the appropriate phone number in the telephone book for her and assured Beth that Barbara would get all the help she needed. She would see to it personally. May reminded Beth that the Navy was one huge family and they would take very good care of their own. Beth was impressed with her. Barbara Copton would be left in good hands.

Despite the late hour, Beth excused herself to contact the base command. She found another phone in the kitchen and called the number at the base. She had to hold on for a while as the call was transferred to an appropriate party. She then explained who she was and why she was calling. Almost as if he received calls like this one every night, the duty officer thanked her for calling, addressed her concerns very calmly, and informed her in sum that Barbara Copton and her husband would receive all the care the massive military organization could muster. Further, a representative from their family services would be at the home at 9:00 in the morning.

When she returned to the living room, finding Barbara and her friend paired off and deep in conversation, Beth suddenly realized that her work was done here for now. She was a stranger in this house once more. That was just as it should be, she thought. So she reminded the two about the appointment in the morning and said her goodbyes. Then following one last hug for the stricken Navy wife, she found the door and slipped out into the night.

Exhausted and exhilarated at the same time, she climbed upon her powerful pony once more, fired it up, and raced a beautiful full moon across the sky.

Chapter 20

Sleep escaped her when she finally fell into bed. Her brain simply would not shut her down for some much needed rest. Instead, she laid wide-awake, tossing and turning, the image of a dead child floating in and out of her consciousness. She plodded into the building the following day without spark and energy, an abrupt change in her demeanor not lost on her compatriots at the office.

Ernie had picked up on it first because Beth had been two hours late getting to work, something she never had done before. He watched her retreat into her office without a morning greeting. He knew she had worked a death case the day before, and he didn't quite know whether to leave her alone or intervene. Later he told Eleanor of his concern.

Eleanor simply walked straight into Beth's office and closed the door behind her. She was not surprised that the room was dark, the only illumination a desk lamp, as the overhead fluorescent light remained off. Beth turned and acknowledged her without a word. Eleanor found a chair, sat, folded her hands, and waited.

Beth turned her back on her for a minute or so, pretending she was reading something. Then she turned with tears in her eyes and spoke.

"Oh, Eleanor, will I ever sleep again?"

"Beth," Eleanor said quietly. "You will never forget it; I told you that once before. You and the mother of that child will continue to share that memory as long as you live. But, in time the sharp edge of the trauma will become dull and less painful. It's our human nature. We must move beyond it. If you don't give it up eventually, you will become permanently injured deep in your soul. Go with it for now. Give the pain its due but only for the time and energy it demands."

They talked for a while about the evening Beth had endured. Eleanor reassured her that soon she would be functioning as normal again. She urged Beth to not stay isolated but to get back into her routine as soon as possible.

"Reach out to your family and friends and hold them close," Eleanor said. "Stay interested in all things going on around you and put your work back into a proper place."

"Truth, Eleanor?"

"Yes," Eleanor replied.

"I really don't have many real friends outside of work. I guess my job and you guys here are all I have, all that I do. I see my parents and most of my siblings at Thanksgiving. Mom and dad live in Omaha now, so far away. Unfortunately they don't seem to understand me. Maybe it's unfair but they don't seem to fully accept me either. My mother keeps asking me if I've found a man and..."

"I've wondered about that myself," said Eleanor with a slight smile, turning the conversation a bit. "Forgive me Beth but ah, is there a guy out there?"

"No, not really. I haven't been dating for years. It is funny that you should ask. I just talked to an old boyfriend on the phone. We were very close in high school, perhaps too close. We have a date set up," Beth responded with a nervous laugh, like the date might be a joke.

"I see," Eleanor said. "You haven't met anyone since high school?"

"Not anyone important."

"What happened between you, if I might ask?"

"I hurt him. I went off to school, and I let him slip away. He's still here in town, a policeman, but he had not contacted me for years. I'm not even sure I want to see him," Beth answered.

"Is it because you really don't like him anymore?" Eleanor asked.

"No, I really can't say that. I was thrilled that he asked me out, and he sounded extremely happy that I accepted. It was almost like we were still in high school. I think I want to see him again, but..."

Beth was quiet for a while. The room was silent except for the regular ticks of a small battery powered clock on her desk. The two women took the brief pause to examine their inner most thoughts. Then Eleanor spoke.

"What's holding you back, Beth?"

"I don't know," Beth whispered. "I guess I'm afraid. I'm still attracted to him. I know that if I get too close... And there's my job. I love what I do..."

"Beth, you probably think I have been prying a little. It would not be unfair to say so. I have a reason, something I want to tell you about myself. Maybe it will help you. Years ago I met a wonderful man. We were happily married for a while, a little over a year. I became pregnant soon after we were married. I lost my baby during childbirth. It happens. But instead of burying my baby and moving on, I buried my husband. I guess I decided it was his fault somehow. I was already working as a social worker and my job, my vocation, was extremely important to me. He came back to me later, wanting to reconcile, wanting to be with me again I kept him on a string for a while because I was so caught up in my work, thinking he could wait, but he broke the string, and I let him get away. I threw myself headlong into my work and committed myself to my clients and my peers," Eleanor said.

"Here's the bottom line, Beth. You should not marry a job. It is not wise to let work consume you. If you do, there can be consequences," Eleanor added.

"If I had to do it all over again, when my husband came back to me, I would gladly run to him. If I were you, I'd curl up in a comfortable chair and think this whole thing through. If you have any honest feelings for this man, don't be afraid to act on them. Go with your heart, Beth. If it leads you to him, don't let him drift away again. If it does not, keep dating. Right now you are one of the best we have here. But, you will serve families and children much more effectively if you have an anchor, a family of your own, a life of your own. Do some soul searching, Beth, but follow your heart."

And with that, Eleanor rose slowly to depart. Beth stood, took a step toward her in the small office and embraced her, holding on, holding on to her like something solid, something strong in the flood waters, sobbing softly.

"Thanks, El," Beth said after a time, pulling out and standing straight. "I guess you have spun your magic with me today. Is there anything else?" she added in jest.

"There's just one more thing, Beth, don't walk by Ernie or any of us again without flashing that beautiful smile."

Lunch that day was a happening. The team wanted to rally around their wounded coworker. So, the noon repast had become a pseudo office party. All but Cletus were in attendance. He stayed behind to man the phones so Ernie could join his friends.

Mr. Bill ended up providing the party's entertainment. In his most comedic style, Bill made fun of himself. With a flat tone of voice he panned himself as he told his story. He had been out to see the lonely woman who had been sexually aggressive with him only a few days ago.

"Why did you do that?" Vickie had asked. "I thought you would be giving her a wide berth."

"The grandfather called me here at the office," Bill answered. "It seems he was getting concerned for Bessie. She had been depressed since the day I was there, and he couldn't shake her out of it. He told me he didn't know where to turn. He practically begged me to go back out there. He said he was afraid she would harm herself. What could I do? Just walk away. I knew I shouldn't do it, but, hey? Would you guys just turn your backs?"

"Oh, I guess not," said Vickie. "What happened?"

"Yea Bill. Did she make a move on you again?" asked Beth happily, while Eleanor seated across the table looked at her and smiled.

"I drove out that evening. When I got there, the grandfather was nowhere to be found. I figured right there and then that I had been set up, but I knocked on the door and went in anyway. Actually Bessie seemed surprised to see me. But to be safe, I sat down in the parlor on a chair, not the couch, and just talked. She did seem to be depressed. I guess we talked for over an hour. Soon she was smiling and laughing a bit. It was almost like I was reconnecting with an old high school friend or something."

"Uh Oh," said Vickie in a sing-song voice.

"What's that supposed to mean?" responded Bill, sounding falsely insulted by the remark.

"Anyway, I did let her serve me a few drinks and... I guess one thing led to another."

"I knew it!" Vickie shouted, banging a fist on the table and disturbing folks at other tables who looked up to see what was going on, and unbeknownst to Bill and his coworkers, tuned in to their conversation.

"I guess I started to see her in a different light," Bill went on. "She really looked good, despite her size. She just took me by my hand and took me upstairs to her room. She was wonderful. Anyway, we sure had a good old time."

"Wow!" Beth said smiling. "Leave it to Mr. Bill to be so thoughtful. You are always the consummate gentleman, so unselfish and so willing to help others."

The group had a good laugh. Some of the eavesdroppers smiled. But Bill was not finished yet. "I have a little more if you will quit giggling so," he said, again with false indignation.

"After we dressed and talked a little longer, I kissed her and left. It was really dark by then and as I approached my car I saw a figure standing by the driver-side door."

"The old man was waiting there to kick your butt again, right?" asked Vickie.

"That's what I thought. Damn, he just loomed there in the darkness like some kind of a night creature. I didn't know what to do. I just froze in my tracks. Then he starts walking toward me. I began to back step toward the porch. I figure his granddaughter would call him off if need be. Then, he hollers out my name, all friendly like. So, I answer. Why he's not mad at me at all. He's delighted. He comes over, embraces me, and slaps me on the back, smiling and grinning like we were long lost friends or something."

"You have to be kidding," said Beth.

"No. He was sincere," Bill went on. "Good job my boy," he says. "You really laid the giggle stick to her. I heard y'all growling and hissing like two wildcats. And my dear granddaughter, she must have hit the high notes at least two times if not three. My man, I couldn't have found anyone better to service her like that if I had tried!"

"Service her!" shouted Vickie, followed by a collective murmur from the diners seated nearby, who just as quickly quieted and leaned closer for more.

"You know what the deal was?" asked Bill of his collagues, about to tell them the answer himself. "The old fellow was truly worried about his granddaughter. I guess at some level he knew she might not pull out of a downward spiral. So he dreams up a scheme to get her laid, and gives me the call. And guess what? I was a very willing participant!"

And at that last declaration, two women seated opposite at another table began to slowly applaud rhythmically, one of the two with tears in her eyes. Soon other bystanders joined in as the beat and the volume increased. Before long almost everyone in the restaurant was happily clapping although many didn't even know why. Bill rose to his feet, threw his head back, stretched out an arm as if to properly acknowledge his admirers, and took an exaggerated bow. Cheers killed the applause as the DCS crew and the lunch bunch joined into a happy salute for the modern day Casanova who had risen to the challenge for a damsel in distress.

Chapter 21

The next day around noon Beth and Jack met face to face for the first time in years in the parking lot of a deli that specialized in excellent Greek food. They did not embrace at first but awkwardly shook hands instead. But Jack took the initiative and pulled her to him and gave her a hug. She didn't mind at all.

They ordered from the luncheon menu and spent almost the entire hour asking about each other's work. It was obvious that the two of them valued their occupations and were happy in their unique roles as public servants. The parallels did not escape them. They actually found a great deal of common ground.

When the check arrived, they were both enthusiastically engaged with each other, sharing again, enjoying the company. So lost in the short reunion, they had barely touched their food. As Jack pulled out his credit card, they both started eating, giggling as they hurriedly packed away some sustenance, like chipmunks filling their cheeks for the winter store. They hugged again in the parking lot but before leaving they agreed to get together again, and soon. Jack suggested the coming Friday night. Beth didn't even blink. That was fine with her but she wanted the tab. She suggested a restaurant near her apartment.

Jack was stoked as he drove back to the station. All his fears had vanished. She had been warm and wonderful, just as before. He chided himself for taking so very long to reconnect with her. What on earth had he been thinking? He did not allow himself to think beyond the next date, but the promise of seeing her again was enough to put him on cloud nine.

As he hiked up the stairs to meet Loomis, he was whistling, something he had not done since he was a teen. Loomis could not help but notice that his partner was grinning like a possum eating a pomegranate.

"Whoa there, Mulk!" Loomis hollered greeting his friend. "Do I notice a little extra giddy-up in your step? You, ah, you enjoyed that lunch date huh? Well good for you and good for me. I hope it all works out for you my man because I am so tired of carrying all the weight while you drag ass around. You need a little charge back in your oh so boring personal life. Wait? You don't have a personal life! Anyway, Mulk, I'm glad to see you smiling."

When Beth got back to her office she started in on the endless task of up-dating the computer. But, her mind kept drifting back to her luncheon date with Jack. It had been fun, and she found herself drawn to him. In all honesty she had to admit that she was truly anxious to see him again. But, the same questions nagged at her. Did she really want to get involved again? What about her independence and the commitment to her job? It was not lost on her that she was wasting time right then and there thinking about him instead of getting her work done

Then in the midst of the struggle to rationalize her way through the issues, she remembered the words of Eleanor Porter. "Follow your heart."

Was it that simple, she asked herself. If she truly followed her heart, she would lay down her concerns for independence and the rest and let the relationship go where it would go. She knew the boy well, and she had loved him dearly. At lunch she met the man, yet he seemed no different than the boy. Was that possible, she mused, or had the years of separation changed him?

Perhaps with a little more time, she would know for sure that he was still her closest friend, her soul mate and, yes, still the one she loved. She smiled knowing that she was now eager to get to that restaurant and find out.

Chapter 22

Later that same day, soon after 5:30 P.M., Cletus finally got shed of an outraged preacher who had come in to see him, demanding that he and his family be left alone.

Vickie was working an anonymous child abuse report that indicated that the preacher regularly beat his two young children, ages five and six, with a thick piece of dowel that left visible slash marks and serious bruises. She had seen the children after school and confirmed it. Further the children seemed fearful and withdrawn when she tried to talk to them. Like abused animals they shied and hung back, not sure if they could trust adults not to harm them. To protect them from further abuse, Vickie had secured a court order to place the kids in shelter care pending final disposition of the case.

The man was hung up on the Old Testament command in Proverbs that required a father to beat his son with a rod to deliver his soul from Hell. He told Vickie that he would continue to discipline his children as he saw fit. Cletus had called him and asked him to come in.

Cletus attended a fairly conservative Baptist church each week with his family. He was accepted and secure even there in his belief that not all the Bible was literally the word of God, although he understood that the majority of the congregation would disagree with him. He simply could not blindly take every word as divine truth. Most people who said they did, seemed to pick and choose what they would accept, ignoring, for example, all the pages of ancient social law and practice that would make it inconvenient for them in the modern era, to say the least. This guy was adamant and told Cletus that he had no authority to stop him from disciplining his children according to his religious beliefs. Cletus had ended the argument by asking the preacher to unzip the leather bound Bible he carried with him and find Matthew 22:19-21.

After the man read the passage, Cletus explained.

"I want you to pay close attention to me, sir. You're looking at Caesar, at least, one of his representatives. Now you can obey Caesar's laws and learn to discipline your children without violence and injury or you can risk having your children placed in foster care for an extended period. The courts will enforce Caesar's law and beating young children, leaving nasty bruises and lash marks on their bottoms and the back of their legs is not only child abuse, it is a crime, and it will not be tolerated. Frankly, you are lucky you are not facing criminal charges for aggravated assault!"

"Render unto Caesar what is Caesar's or face the consequences. Do you understand that?"

"I am not here to receive religious instruction from an untrained lay person," the preacher responded. "I know what my God commands of me. I will pray on this and let you know my decision," the preacher said.

"I want to hear from you by no later than 9:00 in the morning," Cletus advised him. "If I don't, I will have to assume you will continue to use the rod. Then I will take action according to the law and remedy that situation. Just be assured that your children will not be coming home any time soon."

Cletus sat at his desk for a few minutes after the man left. He was proud to say he was a Christian but being one was not easy. Intolerance, violent crime, drug and alcohol abuse, rape, war, and even genocide still raged on in the world resulting in poverty, famine and disease. Some Christians could validate almost any sin even though they had been instructed to love their neighbor as themselves. But Cletus did not lose faith, if indeed he often lost patience and energy. He knew in his heart that most Christians and other people of faith softened the hard edge of human kind. As an old pastor once told him in his youth, if your car broke down late at night on the highway, whom would you like to see drive up, a man who rejected all religions or a man of God?

He suspected that the preacher would not relent, and he would see him in court. It saddened him but he would not condemn the man. Instead he silently offered up a prayer.

Cletus was drained as he walked out the door of the building into the parking lot. Sometimes the job wore on him like carrying a huge drum of water, the contents shifting with every step. This was one of those days. He trudged wearily toward his car. It was parked near the back of the lot. As he approached it, he noticed a man sitting in a pickup, across the street from the lot. He didn't recognize who it was at first. Then, the fellow lifted one hand, a finger extended, and pointed directly at him. It was Leonard Samford.

Almost at the same moment, a shiny black Charger rolled slowly down the street and pulled in behind the pickup truck, engine still running. For a moment no one moved. Then, Samford cranked up his truck and quickly sped away. The tinted window of the driver's door of the Charger slid down silently. Willis peered out and showed himself to his old friend who was still standing in the lot. Slowly Willis raised his hand, holding a handgun. Cletus thought it might be a 9mm Glock. Then as quickly as it had opened the window rose and thumped back into the closed position.

Cletus wanted to approach the car to speak with Willis, but before Cletus made a move the Charger eased away from the curb, rolled slowly down the street, and disappeared.

Chapter 23

They met at an intimate Italian restaurant around 8:00 P.M. She walked from her apartment near by. He drove. They secured a table in a semi private nook near the back.

It was all small talk at first. They had a great deal of catching up to do. They each inquired of family members, friends, and others they knew in common. When the food arrived, they were discussing the years apart, the college work, and more concerning the jobs they loved, interesting cases, and the like. They then started to reminisce about the early days, growing up together, special occasions with the two families, school, and so forth.

The dialogue slowed as they finished up their meal. They had not talked about the one thing that really stood out from all the rest in that stroll down memory lane. It was that particularly crazy and wonderful night that they had dared to break their parents' almost sacred prohibition. It was the night that they absolutely shattered the image others held of them as simply close childhood friends It was the night they ceased being familiar in one sense and yet intimately familiar in another.

Jack had been deeply moved when Beth led him to her bedroom. The two teens had undressed each other and slowly explored each other's body. He had known of her chastity and respected her for it. She had valued her virginity and clung to it as something special while other girls had simply thrown it away. But she had been long convinced that she wanted Jack to have her gift.

Beth was ready in every sense of the word. She had dreamed of it and even in her dreams her body had responded. Jack's unpracticed attempts to caress and arouse her were appreciated but unnecessary. Before they had reached the top of the stairs and flung their clothes aside, she had ached with passion. It was clear to both of them that right there and right then, Jack was to be the first.

And he was. It was a first for him too, but he had a vivid idea of what was in store. He had entered her slowly like exploring a cavern. At first, the passage was warm and inviting. Further in it became dark and difficult. Then with her help he suddenly entered a far chamber. There as she called out his name and held him close, they experienced a breathtaking release. In one moment as lights blazed across thousand of crystals, they cleansed themselves of doubt, fear, and teen anxiety. Their bodies joined, they knew that the one in their arms would be their lover forever.

But, it was not so. They had drifted apart. Their dreams for marriage were put on hold. Then, forgotten. She left the area to attend college at Tulane in New Orleans. She grew there. She matured and her first love, the boy she left behind, began to fade away in her heart. She turned much of her attention to the excitement of learning, new friends, social work, and a new city.

In truth, Beth had had a few short-lived relationships years ago. But they had gone badly, and as she fully delved into her work, she took herself out of circulation without consciously thinking about it. She had grown uncomfortable with the attention she received from men, never sure if they were sincere in their advances or just wanting sex. At twenty-seven she was unmarried and not dating. Perhaps because she turned men away, potential suitors just assumed she was committed to someone else, and they did not pursue her. Down deep Beth was worried that she had thrown up too high a wall. Sometimes alone with her innermost thoughts, she longed for the guy who would just charge into her life and tear that wall down. Every once in a while she imagined that the man might be Jack Mulkey.

Jack stayed in Pensacola, almost exclusively for financial reasons. His parents just could not afford to send him off to Louisiana. He was forced to attend Pensacola Junior College instead. When Beth went away, Jack was crushed. He just could not understand why Beth would want to move, to desert him, and he took it personally. Lacking no logical explanation for the desertion, he blamed himself. He lost sleep. He could barely concentrate on his own college work. He wrote letter after letter begging her for forgiveness for whatever he had done to hurt her. And every once in a while, in the absolute sanctity of his room, he would cry bitter tears. Slowly the wounds healed over, replaced with hardened scar tissue, transforming his aching heart to stone.

Eventually he turned against her. He threw himself into the pursuit of a career. First, he secured an associate degree in criminal justice at PJC. Then he signed on with the Sheriff to become a police officer. While working, he pursued and finally received a BA in Criminal Justice from The University of West Florida. But, she lingered. A strange woman with dark hair flashing by in a car or some snippet of a memory would materialize out of no where to haunt him.

In a vain attempt to strike Beth from his memory forever, he pursued other women. He found himself in four relationships in less than two years. Each had crashed and burned. Over beer one night, his sister had listened to Jack wondering out loud why he could not connect with women anymore.

She had been helpful. "None of them were Beth, Jack. You have not been able to let her go," she added. Instantly Jack realized that his sister was right.

He had run through those relationships one after another not really understanding that he was relentlessly trying to find her. When he finally realized that he was consumed by a dream, he became almost totally disinterested in other women. When Beth returned to their hometown, he didn't have the courage to risk being hurt all over again. He kept his distance. Even though he had been longing for a chance to just talk to her, he feared what she might say. After all, it was over.

After the table had been cleared, they talked on and on. They became more and more open and honest. After all, they were literally old friends who had not seen one another in years. It was easier for them than they may have expected. Like old veterans at reunions, they shared the same stories and laughed once more at the old jokes. Despite the passage of time, they remembered. Despite the separation, they began to reconnect.

After a while the conversation took a turn. Despite everything, both were still carrying a torch. Like the fire carriers of ancient tribes, they had protected an ember, protected it from extinction. Now, in the process of warming to each other, the small flame began to grow. Beth was the first to lay it out on the table.

"Jack," she said quietly. "It sounds like both of us have not exactly moved on. I want you to know something. I have always remembered what we had back then, all the good times. Truthfully Jack, that night we shared was magical, and I will always treasure it like it was the most important experience in my life. I really tried to reinvent our relationship as nothing more than a simple teenage fling. But, now I don't know if I can. It seems to be more than that."

"What?" asked Jack, surprised at what he was hearing.

"I'm not sure what I'm saying, but being with you here seems so right to me. I. I think.... Well, maybe I'm making too much of this," she added quickly.

"Wait a second, Beth. I want you to know something too. I have only seen you around town a few times since you got back from Tulane. What, maybe four or five times in several years? But each time that I saw you, my heart skipped a beat. When you agreed to have lunch and then come here with me, to go out together, I was on cloud nine. I wanted to hate you Beth. I tried very hard. But no matter what, you always ended up right back in a special place in my heart."

Beth recalled what she had told herself a day or so earlier. Let it go where it will go. She now knew where she stood. Jack, the boy and Jack, the man, were one in the same. She closed her eyes, hung her head a little, and let go of all the doubts and fears. She felt her body relax, as years of checked emotions fell away. She literary experienced a physical reaction of sorts, like the realization that a dull headache had gone away, as her mind cleared, and she found herself at peace. When she opened her eyes and looked up at him, tears began to fall. They were not for regret. They were for the absolute joy of certainty.

"You big hunk! You big SOB," Beth said emphatically, tears flooding her eyes. "Don't you see, Jack? Don't you get it? Where have you been? I have been waiting for you. I have been waiting for you to come get me for a long, long time."

They just stared at each other across the table for a while. They looked upon each other almost exactly as they had before as teen lovers. With soft teary eyes and tender smiles, they silently renewed that relationship. Jack's pain disappeared, and Beth's wall came crashing down!

A waiter made an obvious gesture that the restaurant was to close soon. But before either made a move, Beth said in a low almost haunting voice, "Jack, why don't you come over to my place for a while. We can walk from here."

Jack felt a twinge of excitement in his loins. There was no mistaking her intent. A beautiful woman with a body to rival any other, the only woman he had ever loved, was inviting him back into her bed. Without a word, he rose. She did so as well. He went to her and took her into his arms and kissed her long and deep. They both could feel the other's heat. Jack threw down a fifty-dollar bill, not interested at all in change, and they hurried from the place.

They stopped to kiss several times along the street. Both could feel wetness in their thighs as their bodies reacted to feverous stimulation. They paused in a dark storefront. Jack found her breasts through her clothes, and she in turn found him.

"Get a bed for Pete's sake!" a man hollered from a passing car. That cooled the ardor not in the least, but they did hurry on.

After entering the living room of her apartment, she excused herself for a moment and retreated to her bedroom. As she walked away, Jack noted that she was trying very hard to shed her clothes. So he in turn kicked off his shoes and stripped to the skin. He stood as naked as the day he was born staring at the doorway she had entered and waited, panting softly.

And then, there she was. She stood in the doorway, nude, legs apart, hands on hips, her body trembling slightly. Jack started to move toward her. But she raised a hand and stopped him. She wanted to savor the moment, and he understood.

Jack feasted with his eyes and gasped. She was stunning! She was in her prime. Full breasts and toned flesh accented a body sculpted by exercise and diet. Her white skin, reddened in places from excitement, was offset by beautiful black hair, both here and there. There was a glow to her, a glistening all over that seemed to signal that she was ready, more than ready, to give and to receive.

Jack stared at her. He swelled, fully engorged. He longed for her with a primitive passion bred into man down through the millennia. His breathing labored. His heart rate increased. His face contorted with lust.

Beth could not take her eyes off of him. Jack was the statue of David but with one big exception. He was chiseled and strong in build, perfect in proportion, all male. Although she tried to avoid dropping her eyes, she did. It stood firmly erect, bigger than she remembered, wet. Her thighs moved together slightly. She slowly rolled her hips, massaging herself, unconsciously prepared herself for him.

Then, no longer able to stand it, Beth closed the gap between them and flung herself against him. He hugged her crushing her in his arms. They kissed. Then she inched away, reached down between his legs with both hands and grasped him. She moved her hands ever so slightly.

There was a sudden flinch. Jack tried to pull away.

"Oh no," he sighed as his eyes rolled back into his head in the throes of orgasm and his copious discharge splattered against her.

"Jack!" she blurted.

"No. No. No," he kept saying, almost in rhythm, until he was spent.

"Come with me," she said, taking him by the arm. And they both retreated into her shower.

There they slowly took turns washing each other with shower gel and bare hands. Jack kissed her, pulled her against him with both hands on her bottom, lifted her as she flung her thighs around him, and slid her gently up and down over his body. She moaned. The water was warm. Jack was heating up quickly. Beth was already hot!

She turned off the water, hurriedly toweled both of them, and practically ran with Jack in tow to her bed. She pushed him down on his back then lay next to him on her side. She reached for him and fondled him. When he was almost fully restored, she rose and sat on his thighs facing him, her knees straddling his body. She gently rolled herself back and forth against him while continuing to coax him back to where he so proudly stood just a few minutes before. He exceeded her expectations. With eyes drunk with pleasure once more, she lifted her body slid forward and stopped directly over him, probing ever so slightly by raising and lowering her hips, poised to lower her body fully upon him.

But before she could complete the act, she pulled back suddenly and screamed in pain.

"Cramp," she murmured gritting her teeth and flopping off and away, desperately trying to plant a foot on the floor. In so doing however she became tangled in the top sheet and merely fell headfirst part of the way down. Still flailing about, she managed to kick Jack square in the groin, nearly sending him into shock.

"Ahhh," he grunted, while trying desperately to catch his wind and find a place of safety. But in the twisting and turning, they tore the sheet loose and crashed down together in a tight space between the bed and the wall effectively wedging them there. Beth ended up pinned to the floor, her gnarled muscle unrepentant and even angrier than ever. Almost in a panic to relieve the pain, she pushed and hollered for Jack to get off of her. When he could not instantly do so, she screamed again three or four times with more and more urgency. In desperation she finally bit him on the chest.

"OW! OW!" Jack hollered while squirming to get free.

"Get off of me!" Beth screeched, the cramp tightening its grip.

"I'm caught! OW! Damn, will you quit....!"

"GET OFF ME!" Beth bellowed, now almost desperate.

Jack finally found his feet. Beth soon followed, planting her leg and vigorously pounding and massaging the cramped muscle, like an alien creature had taken up residence in her flesh. Jack was checking his chest for puncture wounds when a big man smashed his way through the apartment door. Jack turned to the noise and confronted the invader as the man charged across the living room, a fury in his eyes. Before Jack could do a thing, the man flew into the bedroom and crashed into Jack sending both of them flying in tandem. They landed on the bed, effectively breaking the rails and ended up tussling and wrestling like schoolboys in a playground fracas.

Beth had somehow managed to get out of the way. She was hobbled a little, but soon was up and at them. She picked up a brass bed lamp and waited a second until the intruder, who was on top of her lover, offered up a clean shot at his head. Then, she clubbed him right smack on his crown. The poor fellow rolled off of Jack and moaned. Jack just lay there on the ruined bed, exhausted.

Others had heard the commotion and before Jack and Beth could cover their nakedness, three other men ran into the room. All of them stopped suddenly as if they had been zapped by dog collars crossing an invisible electric fence. Three sets of eyes stared as one directly at the main attraction there. Beth, suddenly realizing that she was as nude as the day she was born, reached for the twisted sheet and draped herself like the Statute Of Liberty.

Still naked, Jack got up and walked right past the three men. They were still frozen in time and space staring at his girl like they had never seen anything like her before. Maybe they never had. Jack found his pants, flashed his badge, and took control of the situation. The men had been playing poker in the apartment below. They had heard strange noises and screams. They thought a woman was being attacked.

The fellow with the lump on his head was not badly hurt, and he actually apologized for breaking in the door. The poker group left in good humor after helping Jack figure out a way to use the bathroom door to secure the entrance while Beth hid in her walk-in closet.

After the guys were gone, the would-be lovers ended up in the living room giggling. All desire for sex was gone, totally gone. They did not speak of it then, but their relationship had fully rekindled. They made a vow to make a go of it. Before leaving however, Jack voiced a different kind of vow. He promised Beth that he would find a perfect time and place for them. They would take it slowly, do it right, and make up for lost time too.

As they kissed to say goodnight, Beth sensed that she could easily get aroused again. Leaning tight against Jack in his embrace, she could also tell that Jack was still very glad to see her.

Chapter 24

Darnell Rogers-Smithson loved his house, a huge, five, bedroom, seven bath symbol of his wealth and power located on Pensacola Beach . He found great pleasure in throwing grand parties there designed to impress his many business associates, friends, and customers. Everyone usually came if invited, all except his loving wife. She was usually a little under the weather and confined to her suite. Some of the guests wondered if she even lived there any more. Two or three of the men knew damn well that she did.

The catered food was the best that could be found in the area, and the host never ran out of booze. Friday evening found him holding forth on a raised deck near the pool with close to one hundred guests partying below. He stood there overlooking the masses with his closest pals and some of their wives, jammed together like the owners and players of a winning Super Bowl Team. Adoring fans, or not, smiled and waved from below.

He was celebrating. His three new car dealerships spread over the Panhandle area of Florida were cash cows. They never seemed to stop producing. They, along with several other ventures, made him a rich man indeed. Plus, he had shoved that unfortunate matter involving the daughter of one of his friends right back into the faces of those who tried to bring him down. His wife had been concerned about that incident, but she never said a word. She simply went about her business satisfying her addiction for clothing, jewelry, antiques, fine cars, and illicit sex.

Darnell was still on top of his game, and he knew it. Before the evening was over, he would have a serious talk with two of his closest business allies in his private den. He was now convinced he should run for office and was actually chomping at the bit to destroy the sitting State Representative who held the seat he wanted. The two, one a brother and another, a cousin, thought that Darnell was an evil Jekyll and Hyde.

They would be overly energetic in support of him, and they would help with campaign financing. Darnell Rogers-Smithson had hired them to help manage those cash cows for him, and they enjoyed great riches too. But, while they would pretend to earnestly kowtow and worship him, they would actually loathe the bastard. These two knew he had raped that little girl because he bragged about it to them. He spoke of it casually, as if he had played a wonderful round of golf. They hated the fact that Darnell felt free to enlighten them because he knew he had them by the balls. They were the worst kind of cowards, they knew it, and they would keep their mouths shut.

Darnell rose early even though he did not retire until 2:30 A.M. He was a high energy individual and could manage on very little sleep. Three hours was almost exactly what he got that night. Usually he was wheeling and dealing before 7:00 A.M. While this was a Saturday morning, he wanted to be in his flagship dealership by 8:00 at least.

He loved to walk on "his" beach. He owned over 500 feet directly on the Gulf of Mexico. He despised the fact that there was a public right away. He had tried and failed to remove it in court. But, it was "his" nevertheless. Often he would simply walk out wearing only a pair of shorts so that he could revel in the coolness of the sea breezes. The sun was just beginning to rise. A low blanket of clouds along the horizon remained in a deep purple while the sky above was beginning to glow orange. He stood and watched as the colors deepened and evolved and than strolled out into the water letting the surf massage his legs.

A jogger in a dark, hooded sweatshirt came loping down the beach at the tide line. Darnell turned angrily to stare down the intruder. Just as he completed the pivot, a piece of lead exploded into his skull right between his eyes, passed through his head, and exited out the back through a gaping hole, followed by a gush of bone and brain. The bullet flew on into the water while the gore sprayed out into an incoming wave. His lifeless body stood for one split second, a dead man walking, then fell backward into the surf. An arm moved gently in the tide to the endless rhythm of the sea, as if Darnell was waving goodbye.

More lead followed smacking into the dead man's guts. Someone wanted to make sure that Mr. Darnell Rogers-Smithson would never strut around on this beach again.

Jack Mulkey and Arthur Loomis got the nod early Saturday morning. Normally they would not have pulled another case so quickly but one of the other investigators who handled murder cases was on vacation in Mexico and another was recovering from an automobile accident. They had Purvis Dickie cooling his heels in jail while they tried to find additional evidence for the prosecutor and awaited lab results. They did not welcome another murder case particularly one which was called in at dawn on a weekend but they soldiered up and moved out when called.

They were rather late getting to the crime scene. Loomis had been shacked up with a bartender who worked in a sleazy joint in Brownsville, far from the side of town for so called respectable folks. Loomis liked her a great deal even though she was a little older than him and rough around the edges. She was as sweet and fun loving alone with him, as she was tough and unapproachable while working behind the bar. She was drawn to him because he spoke with intelligence, treated her as a friend and never once leered at her, stupidly, like she was nothing but a two-bit whore. While Loomis was unattractive because of his face, she really knew what ugly was, and he was none of that.

Jack met Loomis in the parking lot of a nice seafood restaurant by the bay, the kind of place that the tourists loved. Loomis piled in with his partner, and they headed out. Far from the concrete jungle, they arrived at a large curved driveway surrounded by perfect landscaping just as Ed Kambler, the medical examiner investigator, was coming off the beach from the side of the huge three story brick house.

"Mr. Rogers-Smithson is your victim. Found him out in the surf, about six or seven yards out. Heard of him?" asked Ed.

"Yea," grunted Jack, still trying to shake off the sleep. "Car dealer, right?"

"He was shot in the face, straight through the brain. He put at least three more in the belly for fun. The gun had some clout and the shooter may have used hollow points considering the extent of the exit wound. Probably less than two hours ago."

"Who found the body?" asked Jack.

"Wife. Said she heard the shots."

"You kidding me?"

"No. She called 911 sometime after 6:00 A.M. You and Loomis are going to have to figure that one out. Although to tell you the truth, the surf is moderate, and the gun may have sounded like a cannon," replied Ed.

"Do you think there are any slugs in him?"

"I have four entry wounds and only three exit wounds. I may have one inside, but if I were you, I'd get me a metal detector out there."

"Any shells?" asked Loomis.

"Lots of little periwinkles," answered Ed.

"It's too damn early for that, Ed," sighed the big cop.

"None can be seen by the water. I didn't go inside the tape. The team is already at work in there, and they may have something for you. Any other questions?" asked Ed.

The two cops would both think of things they should have asked later, but at the moment they stood silent.

"I'd love nothing more than to stand here in my sand and water logged shoes and my totally ruined clothes, but to tell you the truth, I want to go home, change and spend all day and part of tonight doing my thing so that you heroes can have all the details tomorrow morning."

"That's a deal," growled Loomis, who was still mentally suffering from the effects of coital-interruptus as the blasted cell had ended his second organism a bit prematurely.

A uniform had roped off a large area of beach in front of the spot where the body had been found in the surf several yards from the water's edge. She used a half dozen lawn chairs that she had carted down from the pool as anchors. She was really using her head as footprints were at issue here. The yellow tape, flapping in an early morning breeze served to remind all present that this was a murder scene, ostensibly turning the normally beautiful setting into nothing more than a back alley or a body dump.

The removal people and a Sergeant George Sheffield were marching around the tape with the body when Jack and Loomis walked up. They paused where they met to allow the investigators a quick look. When the investigators had seen enough, they glanced at each other. They both knew without saying that someone had executed the guy with the first shot and then kept pulling the trigger in order to overkill him. It was readily apparent that the killer knew Mr. Rogers-Smithson and hated him in the worst way. They might have guessed as much, but they did not realize then just how long the hate list would become.

"Nice and personal, don't you think," said the Sergeant.

"That or a hit," mused Loomis.

"Loomis, you are forgetting that you aren't in Kansas anymore? We don't have mobsters under every cabbage here," laughed the Sergeant.

"Hell. George. I ain't even been there. You know though, those flying monkeys scared the crap out of me when I first saw that movie. That was freaky, man."

"Loomis, I can't picture you being afraid of anything."

"I'll tell you one thing boys," Loomis said changing the tune, "whoever nailed this poor bastard had no fear. He just walked out here cool as could be and laid him out. He struck him down hard. Whether he got paid for it or not, he damn well wanted that man dead."

"You got that right," said George. "I guess I'll leave it with you guys. Fill me in later when you have some time."

Mr. Darnell Rogers-Smithson was allowed one last stroll around his property. Snug in his body bag, he was taken to the pool area and then across the gorgeous lawn, around the stately mansion to the removal van. The edifice he had erected still stood. But no one would have to stand him, anymore.

Loomis then talked with the cop who had answered the 911 call. The officer had talked briefly to Mrs. Rogers-Smithson. She indicated that the wife met her at the front door. She seemed to be waiting right there as she opened the door immediately. Mrs. Rogers- Smithson, first name Susan, had told the first responder that she had heard several shots, looked out toward the beach, and saw her husband lying in the surf. Then she had walked out close enough to realize that he was dead.

"Did she tell you she saw her husband from the window?" Loomis asked.

"Yes, she did."

"I'll tell you one other thing," the officer added. " I have not worked a murder before so I can't say for sure, but that gal seemed too damn calm. She was cold. Really cold."

Loomis thanked her for her help. He also made a point to jot down her name and badge number. Doing so was routine, in case the officer was needed for testimony later in court. But Loomis had another reason. He wanted to write a note to her lieutenant for her file. Loomis damn well appreciated the fact that the officer had been proactive and taken an extra effort to secure the crime scene.

Jack had been quizzing the crime scene squad. There was one set of footprints coming out to the water's edge that had to have been the victim's. There was no return track. Another set, probably belonging to the wife, traced out from the house, stopped about five yards short of the tide line and returned. There were no bullets or shells to be found in the sand. They were waiting for another tech to arrive in diving gear to search in the surf.

With little more to learn from the crime scene at present, the detectives decided to talk to the wife. They approached the mansion from the rear and were about to climb a massive curving stone staircase that led to the pool area when they spotted Mrs. Rogers-Smithson staring down from above. She was waiting near the top of the stairs when they arrived.

"Mrs. Rogers-Smithson, I am Detective Mulkey and this is Detective Loomis," Jack said by way of introduction, wondering to himself why anyone desired by choice to have a hyphenated name.

"I don't care who you are, but I do understand why you are here," the woman stated, directly with no hint of emotion.

"I am not going to grieve for that bastard. I'm glad he is dead but I did not kill him. Here is a short list of people you may wish to talk with, she went on, handing Jack a hand written list. I am just one member of that hate group. I have spoken to my attorney and our conversation is over. Are you prepared to arrest me?"

"Not today." Jack shot back. "But you and your attorney will no doubt see us again. Thank you for your time."

Without another word, Mrs. Rogers-Smithson turned on her heels like a soldier and marched, fully erect, back into her mansion.

After hanging around for a time hoping the techs would find a shell casing or two, the investigators plopped into Jack's vehicle.

"There's a stone cold woman." Loomis growled. "But I have a feeling she didn't pull the trigger."

"Why is that?" asked Jack.

"I don't think she cared enough, one way or the other."

"Let's get out of here before the media gets wind of this story," Jack said as he cranked up his Cherokee. They will be all over the Sheriff too so we better alert the brass to stand by for a quick briefing."

"I'm dialing now," said Loomis.

On the way back across the Three Mile Bridge, the partners remained silent, each deep in thought. It was Jack who spoke first. "Did it occur to you that we have had two very violent, up front and personal murders here in less than two weeks?"

"I was just thinking about the same thing. We usually don't have more than thirty murders a year in this county. Now we get two rather rare personal overkills one right behind the other," answered Loomis.

"But they are really different, right?" said Jack, more as statement than a question.

"Yeah," whispered the big guy. "We have Little Dicky locked up for the first one. This one can't be his thing. But, you know, he may not have done the McCanless woman. That little prick still doesn't look right to me. I don't think he has the chestnuts to slit someone's throat. Do you?"

"We are definitely on the same wavelength. I've been bothered by how easy it was. Why would a stone cold killer leave the knife for us to find? Basically he even gave us written permission to go get it," Jack mused.

"I know," said Loomis. "The prosecutor is still working on just how he is going to proceed on that one. He didn't think this case was a slam-dunk that's for sure, and he really wants us to get more evidence. Plus, there's the question of a motive. Before he makes a definite decision, let's talk to Purvis one more time," said Loomis.

"You know he has been asking to see me," Jack said. "Why don't YOU drop in on our little friend? He has always had nothing but nice things to say about you, and I'm sure he would be very excited to see you again."

"Hmmm. The bad cop routine. You may have something there. I'll be glad to visit with the little cockroach, although I know he would really prefer that it be you instead. I hope he won't be too disappointed," said Loomis jokingly.

"He really does need to learn a few social graces," concluded Jack. "The visit will give my little pal an opportunity to apologize to you for those unwarranted remarks he made about your heritage."

"You are so right, Ollie," Loomis said playfully.

Chapter 25

Jack and Loomis had been swept up into the whirlwind of the Rogers-Smithson case from the moment their briefing began with the Sheriff. He took responsibility for any and all news contacts, scheduled coordination meetings throughout the next few days, and made assignments. All knew that the murder as news would fade in a few days, at least until there was an arrest. But, the feeding frenzy of attention had to be carefully fed or the good guys risked getting bitten themselves.

The main focus for the two detectives was the list Mrs. Rogers Simpson had given them, the Murder Club, as Loomis called it. There were sixteen members of the club. The widow had included herself right at the top of the list. Down near the bottom, number fifteen, was the name Marcus Velney.

They jumped into the task of interviewing the Murder Club members with both feet but secretly wondered if the wife had just handed them a perfect way to throw suspicion on others. Actually after only five interviews, they began to believe that Mrs. Rogers-Smithson was spot on. Two of the four people they saw made no qualms about it. They were happy that the Wicked Witch was dead. Another wasn't quite so effusive, but obviously did not like the victim at all. The last two were interviewed in the presence of their high priced attorneys and actually said very little. Of course that in itself seemed to make the point as well. All seemed to have alibis. Four of the five were home in bed with the wife. The other should have been sleeping in his own bed but had somehow managed to concoct a late hour lie for the wife and bedded down with the girlfriend instead.

Loomis dropped by the jail Monday evening late to visit with Little Dicky. He had arranged though a friend to have the suspect delivered to a small interview room in the administration section of the jail compound that was normally locked up tight after 6:00. It contained a tiny steel desk and two chairs, a safe place for the business staff to talk with a prisoner now and then. There was a small slit window near the ceiling. Loomis turned the light out and let the fading sun do what it could to illuminate the space. The gloomy transformation suited his needs perfectly. Loomis settled down to wait.

Soon a correctional officer opened the door and pushed in a dour looking leprechaun in an orange jump suit, one Purvis Dicky.

"Hey, Martin," said Loomis, "how's it"… But before he could complete his greeting, Martin's prisoner tensed and recoiled in horror.

"Noooooo! No way!" screamed the little man like someone being dragged before the gallows.

Thinking that his charge was going to give him trouble, the officer threw Purvis into the vacant chair. Before the little guy could recover, the officer then slammed most of his weight onto him to hold him still long enough to secure him. Despite much wiggling and whining from his charge, he managed to cuff Purvis to a steel bar that had been bolted into the wall beside the desk. Loomis just sat calmly with his hands folded in a pyramid enjoying the sideshow.

"This police officer beat me. He beat me! You can't leave me alone with him!" Purvis wailed. "I have rights. I want to see my attorney. This man is crazy. Let me out of here. Or stay here with me! Please...."

Loomis rose slowly out of his chair and reached across the table. Purvis, screaming for help, tried to shrink and disappear into the chair. Because of his size he did a very good job of it too. Then, with one smooth move, Loomis put his middle finger to his thumb, put a little pressure on it, and then released it with an audible whack on the rim of Purvis Dicky's ear.

"SHUTUP!" Loomis roared.

Several doves roosting nearby rose and flew quickly into the night sky. Purvis and the correctional officer froze in position bug-eyed and silent. Several convicts housed across the way jumped to attention at the powerful command and shut their yaps. It was reminiscent of a scene in an old Bob Newhart show whereby a huge Black man screams "Sit Whitey!" at his pale dog and all the White folks in the room immediately find a chair!

When it became possible to hear again in the little echo chamber, Loomis picked up the distinct sound of sniveling, a cross between sniffing to keep mucus from running down his nose and weeping.

"They sure don't make many hard cases anymore do they, Martin?" asked Loomis of the correctional officer.

"Oh, they bad on the street, now. They can sell those wolf tickets, can't they? They're real men on the playground and in the back alleys. They are true thugs! Uh Huh! Unless, of course, their Mommas catch them talking trash. This guy is full-grown and crying like a baby."

"Oh, this one's a piece of work. He had something awful to say about my mother. I thought I might teach him some manners," replied Loomis.

Hearing that, Purvis made one last attempt to find a way out of the room. "Mr. Correction Officer. Please! Please take me back to my cell. I'm telling you that this man will beat me. I am afraid for my very life," he said as sincerely as he could be.

But seeing that Martin was intent on leaving him with Loomis, Mr. Dicky reverted to form.

"You sonbitch. I'm going to report you to the Sheriff. You are going to lose your job over this. You hear me you old bastard? I'll file charges with the FBI. They…"

"Just holler when you are finished talking to this idiot," said Martin. Then he turned; walked out the door, and closed it with some authority, the bang sounding like a shotgun blast in the empty halls.

Purvis froze, anticipating trouble. Loomis sat back in his chair, saying nothing. He just listened for a minute or two as his friend Martin made footfalls walking down the hall. The sounds of a door being unlocked, opened, closed and relocked reached him followed by more footfalls trailing away.

Fear gripped Purvis as he tried some mental gymnastics to deal with his situation, but thinking clearly wasn't his strong suit. There in the relative quiet and the failing light, sitting with a wild unpredictable cop, his small mind churned away like an old computer on broadband trying to download a huge file. It wouldn't compute. In truth he didn't know whether to fish or cut bait. So he tried begging again. But before he could get a word out, Loomis shattered the peace with another ear splitting demand for silence.

Finally after another few minutes, Loomis spoke. "I need to know the truth. You do know what truth is, don't you?"

"Yes sir," snapped Purvis like he had been addressed by a commanding officer.

"Did you kill Milly McCanless?"

"I swear to you, Mr. Loomis. I didn't kill her," Purvis said rather softly befitting the change of tone in the room.

"Do you know who would do such a thing?"

"I've asked myself that a lot. She was into hurting herself. She didn't need nobody to do that for her. Honestly I don't even have a guess who it might be."

"Do you know who might have fathered the baby girl?"

Purvis didn't even blink. "She was a few days short of forty when she had that kid. She never used anything. I wouldn't know. I guess you could say she slept with anyone who give her a few bucks. Could be ten, twenty men, for all I know."

"Good. Now tell me everything that happened that night. Tell me every detail. Pretend you and I are watching a movie of you, and I am blind. Tell me about each and every scene," Loomis instructed.

After a dozen failed attempts to get started in the level of detail Loomis wanted, Purvis seemed to get the idea. Sensing he was actually talking with real purpose to a policeman, who was keenly interested in what he had to say, he babbled on like an excited schoolboy. Later when Loomis thought he was ready for it, he pressed Purvis hard about his feelings too, not just his movements and activities. It was not easy with Purvis. He didn't seem to understand the concept of feelings. When he finally asked Purvis if he liked the murder victim, he actually surprised the veteran cop with a revealing show of emotion.

"Listen I. Ah. I. I aint much. I aint no good with women," Purvis began. "I guess you could say I am ugly. Least ways, that's what they all say behind my back. I can't find no jobs neither. But Milly didn't never say a word about that. Sure I paid her. Most times at least. But she was kind to me. And that night I had a little money, and we had a good time. We went back to her place and just crawled in bed like real folks do. See she had troubles too. She had been into crack and booze. She accidentally smothered her baby sleeping with it on a couch. She lost two other kids to the welfare folks. She said they couldn't trust her to take good care of them. Milly was messed up after that, you know, not right in the head. She stayed high most of the time. But that night for a little while we were just like real folks. Y'unnerstan' what I'm saying?"

Loomis parroted the little guy. "You said you weren't very good looking and had trouble finding a girl friend. But Milly didn't mind and you liked her."

"Yea, that's kinda what I said," Dicky muttered, his head bowed low. "Look at me, Purvis," said Loomis. "Look at me good. Do you think I might just have some idea of what you're talking about? Huh? Do you?" Loomis boomed.

Little Dicky's tiny eyes widened as he stared at the big cop only inches from his broken nose. He didn't quite understand what he had been asked. Then, there in the scars on Loomis' face left by a beer bottle years ago, he finally got it. Purvis was looking directly at a reflection of himself.

"I think so," he said softly. "Neither one of us is a pretty boy. We're more the tough guy type," Dicky offered cautiously.

"That's right, Purvis. I understand exactly what you have been saying. I've been there too. When a man speaks from his heart, he rarely tries to hide the truth," Loomis said with feeling.

"One more time, my friend," Loomis asked quietly. "Did you kill Milly?"

"No, Officer Loomis, I wouldn't done that to her. She was my friend."

"Good!" Loomis followed. "I think that came from your heart."

"You believe me?" asked Purvis hopefully.

"I think so. Let's talk some more." And they did for a time. Before Loomis called Martin and had Purvis put back into his cell, he asked him who would try to frame him by putting the apparent murder weapon in his car.

"Honestly, I can't think of no one. No one knows me very well. No one really sees me. I guess to be honest no one gives a shit about me neither. Maybe I was just there. You know, a trash can for the knife," Purvis responded.

"I have to run Purvis but I want you to know something," Loomis said in wrapping it up. "You are still a little prick. And I am still a cop. Nothing much has changed. But, I don't think you did this, and I will try to figure out who did. One more thing, clean up your act. You still smell like week old road-kill."

"Yeah, Officer Loomis. And you still belong in a zoo," Purvis shot back with a slight smile on his face, hoping he would not be killed. And, he wasn't.

Chapter 26

Cletus assigned Vickie a neglect case soon after she arrived for work Tuesday morning. She was actually on time for a change, and she made sure Cletus noticed. He asked her if she was feeling OK.

Although the report was not coded for an immediate investigation, she wasn't ready to tackle the mountain of paper work that awaited her and decided to just get out for a little while and handle it. Apparently Rufus and Marjorie Johausen were having some problems with a newborn. The report came from a neighbor who would accept a call from the investigator but wanted to remain anonymous. Vickie appreciated this. From her experience this kind of reporter usually knew the family and was concerned about something but wanted to remain in a position to help out if necessary. Openly reporting someone often led to the end of a relationship.

A phone number was provided so she made a call. Vickie introduced herself and thanked the woman for her concern. She added that often people were reluctant to make a report, and the child suffered as a result. Apparently the caller lived next door to the family that consisted of two very young parents and a month-old baby boy. She described two recent visits. Both times the young mother was having difficulty nursing the child, and she really didn't seem to know how to handle an infant.

The husband was proud, perhaps overly proud. He had rejected help from an outreach service that followed up with concerns the hospital staff may have documented. Seems he was determined to prove that he could provide for his family, perhaps to silence parents or others who went ballistic when the girl became pregnant.

The caller was not sure how old they were. She guessed that the girl was eighteen. She wasn't sure about the husband but swore he was much younger, perhaps as young as sixteen.

Vickie rolled through the city streets until she found the small apartment building where the youngsters and their baby were housed. She knocked on the door of their apartment several times. She could tell someone was inside, because she could pick up snippets of whispered conversation through the thin, hollow core door. The people inside were hoping she would just go away.

After a minute or two of knocking without results, she called out and identified herself as an investigator with the Department of Children's Services. She heard a few more whispers, waited, and was about to change her cheerful friendly tone, when the door flew open.

Vickie stood face to face with a clown.

The husband, she assumed, was in clown make-up head to toe. He apparently shaved his head and covered it and his face entirely with white face paint. Then he added a shock of long, bright yellow hair, about the size of a scalp an Indian might have taken, and glued it right on the top of his dome. He had donned an over sized blue nose and had fashioned a clown face with red, black, and yellow paints. It looked as if he had copied someone, because the face looked familiar. In addition he wore a baggy white shirt with wide blue and yellow stripes and a pair of shorts that had been cut off below the knees with a pair of pinking shears. Finally he sported a pair of floppy blue clown shoes that had to have been purchased at a clown supply store.

Vickie had to admit that this clown looked like a clown.

She had to invite herself in, and she promptly did so. Without a word from the clown or the girl sitting on a sofa, she introduced herself again and quickly pretended to guess the names of the pair. Finally the clown invited her to sit on a tall stool that he pulled from a corner. Then he moved across the tiny living room and sat down next to his wife.

Vickie climbed up on the perch and tried rungs one and two to see which position for her feet gave her the best chance for comfort. She wished silently that she had worn a longer skirt so she could at least achieve a degree of modesty. When settled she stared down on the couple feeling just a little bit like a bad girl at school. All she needed was a dunce cap.

She quickly sized up the young wife. She wasn't sure that she was anywhere near twenty. She wore an old Saints T shirt and a pair of faded blue jean shorts. Her hair was a tangle of pale blonde. Her face, arms, and legs were very thin. She wore what proved to be an almost permanent, worried look on her face.

Vickie opened the conversation by simply asking how the baby was doing, like she was an aunt or someone, just stopping by to see the newborn.

The clown spoke. "Fine. We are doing Fine."

Somehow, Vickie knew that sooner or later she was going to crack up. Here she was sitting on a stool like a trained poodle, talking about what many would consider a fairly serious matter, with a clown, for crying out loud.

So, she tried to avoid that embarrassment by addressing this clown business straight on. "Why are you dressed like a clown?" she asked, completely changing the subject.

"I am a clown," he answered.

She felt a slight giggle in her throat but stifled it immediately.

"I guess I know that," she went on. "But why are you dressed up like a clown now?"

"I have a job," he responded quickly.

"Good," Vickie said, not sure if he answered the question or not.

"Do you mean that you are going to be performing somewhere?" she asked.

"Yes, at an office birthday party. I make balloon animals too."

"O.K.," she offered, picturing this clown making a purple giraffe or a pink puppy for the gang at her office. She had to squelch a smirk and was still not sure if she could talk to this clown without blowing snot through her nose in a fit of laughter.

Returning to the point of her visit, she carefully addressed why she was there. There was some concern that the mother was struggling with the newborn. The clown took umbrage and got a little hot under his Donald Duck collar. He wanted to answer and argue the point but Vickie wouldn't let him. She told him with authority that she wanted to hear from the girl. Immediately the young mother started crying.

Now, Vickie was confronted with both a sobbing little Mom and a hostile clown with a permanent smile on his face. She barely kept her composure. Like a kid in church with the giggles boiling up inside her during the Lord's Prayer, she almost cried real tears trying desperately to keep her mouth shut.

Vickie stayed on task while allowing the girl to regain her composure. While the wife sobbed she was able to get some additional information from the clown, and she checked the baby. Soon she had the situation in the home figured out. The baby was fine, but not so the parents. The pair was very young. He was barely seventeen and she eighteen. Understandably they were a tad immature. The young family was isolated as well. The grandparents blamed each other for the unexpected pregnancy and hasty marriage to avoid having the child born out of wedlock. After many squabbles between all parties, the husband had demanded that he and his wife be left alone, and they were.

Marjorie Johausen was clueless about breast-feeding. Even though she had been given instructions in the hospital by two different representatives of La Leche, she was still having difficulty nursing. She was probably suffering from postpartum depression as well, no doubt complicated by her husband's insistence that she didn't need any help.

As Vickie wrapped up her probe, the clown continued to speak for his wife, indicating that all was well. The girl, now quiet, just sat, hands folded in her lap, staring at the floor. Vicky reminded the clown that she wanted to hear from his wife. A pause ensued. Then the girl spoke for the first time.

In a weak and trembling voice she said, "I don't feel right. I love my baby but she is always crying. Rufus, I think I would like to have my mother stop by once in a while."

Rufus! Vickie thought to herself, the actual sound of the boy's real name jiggling her funny bone again. Damn she thought, this kid was destined to be a clown. But she snapped out of it when the young father blew off his wife's request and indicated once more that they could make it on their own.

Vickie became angry at that point. She turned on him and laid down the law. But, it was not easy. She could not look at the floor or the ceiling while lecturing this clown. She had to look at his clown face. She lambasted him, all the while just a hair's breath away from lunacy. His wife needed help, and he had to support her by allowing folks into the home that could provide it. She indicated that she would recommend that her case be closed with voluntary services including nurse visitation from the Health Department as long as he would not stand in the way. If he did, she would petition the court and force the issue.

The boy stood up. Vickie thought he might be growing defensive and more hostile. But, he was crest fallen and defeated instead. In truth he had seen the light, and it had exposed him. He had been stubborn and in the way. He loved his wife and child more than anything else in the world, but he had been stupid. Silently he nodded that he was in agreement, but he hung his head as he did so.

Vickie spotted that gesture immediately. She decided it was time to ease up on the boy. After all he was very young, and he was trying. She looked the clown right into his grossly made up eyes and told him that she was proud of him. She followed that up by congratulating him. He was working. He had a home, and he was doing the best he could to provide for his family despite the hardships.

Unexpectedly, the clown started to cry. The tuft of highlight yellow hair on the top of his head flopped up and down as the sobs came. Tears began to track and smear the makeup. The clown wept.

That was it for Vickie. She now had a silly faced clown standing directly in front of her in full costume, bawling like a baby.

Vickie almost went cross-eyed fighting for composure. She was now in a hushed audience listening to a string quartet softly playing a beautiful concerto. She was now at the ordination of a priest at the most poignant moment in the ceremony when he lies prone at the altar giving himself to God. She was now at a funeral filled with respectful mourners as the tearful spouse lovingly remembered her husband. She was about to die!

Then no longer able to contain it, Vickie burst a gut. She lost all composure, and she laughed. She bellowed and guffawed like Carol Burnette losing it in a skit with Tim Conway. There was no today and no tomorrow, just the moment. Vickie bent over, grabbed her tummy, and howled.

The young parents stared at her with tears of their own, still in their eyes. They stared with eyes wide open in astonishment. Neither could speak. Neither understood.

Vickie's eyes were now clouded with tears, her body wracked with spasms of mirth. She was beyond caring what they, or anyone else for that matter, thought about her to say the least.

It was the young mother who started it at first. She too began to giggle. Then, the boy followed suit. Somehow that just set Vickie off again. Soon all three were just plain lost in it all, like members of an audience who were watching great comedy, the Penguin going after the Blues Brothers or Cato attacking Inspector Clouseau.

It ended finally and for no apparent reason, the three hugged each other like long lost friends.

"Wow, I'm sorry about that," Vickie said. "I just don't usually talk to a clown like that."

"It's all right, Miss Snow," said the girl. "Rufus is a really good clown, isn't he?"

Chapter 27

"I can't let you do this," said Cletus.

"Listen, Cletus. I appreciate your concern, but I have to do it. Leonard Samford scared me. He really scared me. He threw me like a novice rider. I have to get up and get back on. Don't you see?" said Shanice softly.

"No way and that is that. It's too dangerous," responded Cletus with authority.

"I've asked Beth to go with me. She is no shrinking violet, that girl. I've seen her do a karate demonstration. We have to make a home visit. It will be dicey enough recommending foster care without a period of in-home supervision, let alone without a single home visit to give the parents a chance. I want these kids to have a life without fear. If I can't do that for them, I have no business working here. Further, if you insist in trying to stop me, if you force me to remain a coward, I have no business working for you."

"Damn, Shanice. You always try to play that card, don't you? Well, I'm tired of it. Quit if you have to but don't lay that on me. I'm just thinking about your safety. That man is dangerous. At least let me go with you. If something were to happen to you or Beth, I couldn't live with myself."

"Come on, Cletus, think about it. You walk in there, and we won't even get a chance to talk to him or his wife. You will do nothing but serve as a lightening rod, and you know it."

"Shanice, I'm warning you."

"Listen, Cletus, the appointment is for 4:00, and it's already 3:10. We do have a drive you know. I wasn't even going to tell you. I knew you would want to protect me. And I really appreciate the fact that you care so much for all of us. But you know better than I do that you can't stop me. I'll call the moment we arrive at his house and again as soon as we leave, I promise," Shanice said.

"I'll get a uniform to go with you."

"Cletus, we will be fine. Besides, I think Beth could out fight most of those guys when it comes to that. And, I almost hope that sucker tries something."

"You are not listening to me, Shanice. I'm telling you not to go," Cletus said gruffly. Shanice looked at him with some astonishment. "I'm not a little girl, Cletus, and I'm going."

She turned and walked out the door without further comment leaving her supervisor stewing. At one level he understood why Shanice felt she had to go. At another, he was furious with her for putting herself and Beth in danger.

Cletus picked up his cell, found the name Willis in the contact list, and hit the call button. He got voice mail and hung up without leaving a message.

They were running a little late so Beth pushed the Mustang through the city sliding through the manual transition effortlessly. She and Shanice arrived at the Samford home about five minutes early. Beth slammed her door as she got out on purpose to make sure the folks knew that they were there. Shanice led the pair to the cinder block that made up the entranceway to the colorless trailer. Leonard Samford met them at the door wearing nothing but a dirty pair of shorts and that badass sneer. Beth, seeing him for the first time, assumed correctly that he might just want to give her karate training a real world test but that didn't bother her in the least.

"Looky here, Shasta," Leonard said to the shadow of a woman behind him. "They sent that same tar baby back here. Plus a looker too."

Shanice could feel the heat rise on her neck, but remained calm.

Looking past Shanice to Beth, Leonard said softly with intended sex in his voice, "You can come in while your soul sister waits in the car. She ain't welcome here but you can come anytime you want."

"Let's make something clear here, Mr. Sanford," Shanice said. "We need to sit down with you and your wife in your home and discuss plans for the children. I know you want them back. You have made that clear. But they won't come back home just because you say so."

"Whoa, listen to that shit, Shasta. You ain't been a good mother," he sneered.

"Come in here if you want. Both of you. Leonard and I will serve tea and crumpets," the wife said. Then without another word from Leonard, he and his wife stepped back into the doublewide leaving the door open.

Shanice looked at Beth. Beth nodded. They went in.

They entered a dark, damp living room of sorts. It smelled of cigarettes, beer, and spoiled food. The Samfords stood near a kitchen off that room and pointed to a small couch. It looked like it had been hastily cleaned, but not in the normal sense. Off to the side of the couch, items of clothes and other things lay scattered on the floor, like someone had just dumped the mess off the couch so the guests would have somewhere to sit.

"Welcome to our castle, ladies," announced Leonard with half a smile. But somehow that curled lip of his turned that expression into more of a threat than a greeting.

"Have a seat," he said cheerfully, and despite fears of what may be hiding in it, the two parked themselves carefully on the very edge of the tattered sofa.

"Can I get you something," Shasta asked, again with the sarcasm. As she did, both guests looked at her for the first time out of the shadows and were sickened by what they saw. Leonard's bride could have belonged to Frankenstein. Her face was puffy, red and streaked with scars. A fresh abrasion decorated her chin. Even though she wore a baseball cap, there appeared to be clumps of hair missing. She tried to hide what was left of her teeth but couldn't mask the fact that few remained in front. She was obviously a victim of violent physical abuse, awful and often.

Beth spoke first and directly to the point. "Mrs. Samford, how did you get those injuries to your face?"

"Fuck you!" the woman roared. "You come in my house like some kind of debutante cheerleader and try to stir up something? I fell down last evening, that's all. Besides, what I do in my own home is none of your fucking business."

"Hold on now, Honey," Leonard said. "The girls just want to know about our married life. I think it's been awhile since they got any, and they're jealous."

"Mr. Samford. We came here to discuss plans for the children. Could we please quit the games and get on with the important matters," Shanice offered.

"Listen, Aunt Jemima," Leonard said roughly. "I got nothing to say to you."

Then looking straight at Beth he went on. "When do we get the children back?" he asked her.

"Look. The children were removed from your care for child endangerment. This was not the first time you have been involved with a child welfare agency either. We know about several child neglect cases from Alabama. You both have a history of intoxication and violence, and you will not be getting your children back into this home until you are willing to work with us to address the parenting issues that concern us," Shanice answered even though Samford was still looking at Beth.

Slowly he turned away from Beth and faced up with Shanice, a thoroughly disgusted look on his face. "Listen, bitch, and listen good," Leonard muttered softly with the most threatening voice he could muster. "You aren't just walking out of here with that crap. Do you understand me?"

Beth rose from the filthy couch. "That sounds like a threat, Mr. Samford."

"Oh, I think you hear very well. You sit your ass back down there and tell me when my kids are coming home. Or maybe you will be a little late getting home yourself."

Shanice stood as well. Beth, sensing real danger, took one small step toward Samford to give herself a little room.

"We will be leaving now. We don't have anything more to learn about you," Beth said solemnly.

With that, Leonard struck out with his palm in an attempt to push Beth back onto the couch. In a flash, Beth snatched his hand, grabbed him in a wristlock, and sent him directly to his knees hollering in pain.

"As I said, Mr. Samford, we will be leaving now," Beth said. "If I even sense a hint of another threat or any attempt to stop us, I will lay you out on this floor with some serious pain. That is a promise."

With that, Shasta made a move toward Beth. Shanice immediately stepped right in front of her. " Back off and do it now!" Shanice warned. And the battered spouse of Leonard Samford did as she was told. Later, Leonard Samford would punish her for the offense.

"Jesus," Samford moaned, his wrist near the breaking point. "Just get the hell out of here."

"Thanks for your time," Shanice said as Beth gingerly released her lock and the two stepped carefully around him to the door.

"By the way, we will be recommending that your children be placed in foster care. I will be back in touch with you later to explain what we will want as court ordered conditions for their possible return. Try to remember that your life style and behavior are the reasons that they cannot be returned to you at this time. If I were you I'd start with mental health counseling and anger management as soon as possible."

"Kiss my ass," Leonard Samford said meekly from his knees on the floor, vigorously massaging his wrist.

Shanice had forgotten to call Cletus when they arrived. She phoned and reported in, explaining what had happened with an air of joy and excitement in her voice as Beth sped into a curve and flew out of it, hair flying in the wind. Cletus was genuinely relieved but still angry that the two had ignored him.

Chapter 28

Cletus grabbed Shanice and Beth as soon as they arrived at work the next morning.

"Don't get started on anything else. We have to talk," he said. Without a word they assembled in his office.

"You two put me in a position that really was not fair to me. I am your supervisor, and you owe me some respect. I will follow this meeting up with a written warning that will spell out in detail my concerns and my specific orders relative to your responsibility in future, dangerous situations such as this. If either one of you pulls something like that again, I will take necessary disciplinary measures."

"You don't need Beth in here," Shanice said." I didn't let her know you didn't want us going out there."

"Shanice, you did discuss it with me. Cletus, I went out there knowing full well we did not really have your approval," Beth offered.

"I know damn well you did," Cletus followed.

"Look, Cletus. I will take any punishment you want to dish out. I apologize for talking the way I did. I can be very bull headed you know. But, please, hear me out now. I have something very important to say. More to the point, I want you to freely accept what I am about to tell you and take it to heart."

"Oh, really? You want me to listen to you but you just dismiss me like I wasn't even here," said Cletus, still steaming.

"Please, Cletus. Hear me out. It's important to both of us."

"OK. But if you're going to threaten me with your resignation again, I don't want to hear it. You can just write it up and put it on my desk. I told you that I've had it with your game and I mean it."

"Beth, stay with us if you want, but I will be speaking for myself, a Black sister to a Black brother," said Shanice.

"Wow," said Beth. "Can I sit in if I promise to keep my mouth shut?"

"Yes, you sure can," said Shanice. "The more I'm around you the Blacker you get anyway, girl," she added with a smile.

"Here's my point, Cletus. You and I let that bastard scare us. You and I shuffled and jived ourselves right into a safe little corner somewhere. I didn't know what it was. I thought we feared him because he was so openly threatening and violent. But last night I came to a better conclusion. We were afraid of that punk because he made us fear him. Think about it. He hasn't done a thing but shoot off his filthy mouth. He didn't even fight the cops. Why, because they would have bruised his ego to say the least. He is having a huge kick because he has lots of folks, including you and I, looking over our shoulders."

"I am not afraid of that man," retorted Cletus.

"Bull, Cletus!" snapped Shanice. "Remember, I'm speaking to you as a sister to a brother. We have to be honest with each other. We were both trembling in our boots. He is a throwback to those days that our grandparents told us about. He is a hooded nightrider with a rope that rode through our dreams and chased us into the shadows. He knows it too. The pathetic little thug must be defining himself with this act."

"Here's the bottom line, Cletus. Beth, my White sister here did not even blink. Yes, she knows how to defend herself. But, there is more, I promise you. She didn't grow up with any trace of inferiority. She just grew up. When she entered that house, she entered the house. She didn't drag all kinds of baggage in with her. She saw a mouthy punk. I saw a monster."

Cletus didn't respond this time. Secretly he was thinking about Willis, the man he hired to defend him. Shanice had struck home, hard. He, the giant, hard- nosed football star, had let Leonard Samford make him a coward.

Shanice summed up. "Do you know when I figured it out, Cletus? It was the wristlock. Beth slapped on him. Samford wasn't fueled up with Meth or liquor. He had no guts without the juice flowing in his veins. She put him to the floor. And there, like a bad boy being spanked by his mother, he whined and cried like the sissy he really is under all that bravado. I wish you could have seen it."

"Beth," Cletus said. "What your take on Samford?"

"Really, Cletus, I didn't do anything you or Shanice couldn't do. I carry myself with confidence because of my training, but she has it right. I think if Shanice were alone and had just torn into him face to face like she can do, he would have melted. And you, Cletus, could easily have broken that man in two. There's no strength in him, at least as I could tell, he didn't even try to resist."

"So, Shanice , where does all this lead us?"

"Cletus, I almost turned my back on those children the day after I bumped into that jerk. I almost ran away because I was scared. All of us get weary of the nonsense that seems to come with this job. But we can't let anything divert us from our responsibility here. The three of us, the rest of our team, and all of the investigators scattered around this country need to keep on keeping on. That's it."

"Why do you gals always have a way of disarming me? What is it about women anyway? You talk about fingernails, shampoo, facial cream, clothes, and shoes all the time. But when something important and relevant comes up, you always speak the truth. And then, I find myself learning from you instead of the other way around."

"Don't sell yourself short, Cletus," said Shanice. "You always respect us. You always listen. You give all of us the chance to grow. Besides you have the best unit in Florida. Maybe the entire country," she added.

After the women had left and Cletus had an opportunity to hash it all out, he picked up the phone and called Willis. He got voice mail again but this time he left a message. He asked Willis to meet him around 5:30 behind the parking lot.

Willis was already parked in the black Charger when Cletus arrived.

"Willis, you have really helped with this. But I want to call you off. A couple of the women on my staff taught me something this morning. Basically they told me that I had let a punk get under my skin," said Cletus, after he was comfortably ensconced in the passenger seat.

"Cletus, I've known you a long time. You aren't normally afraid of anyone. But they are right. Remember when he was waiting for you here by the parking lot a couple of days ago? I went over to his house that night and had a little talk with him."

"What?" said Cletus, totally stunned.

"I figured it two ways. First, I had no business carrying heat. I'm a convicted felon on parole. I get caught with that bad boy in my pocket, and I'm going back for more hard time. But, I had to end his game one way or the other. So I decided to get inside his head and make him see the light," explained Willis.

"But listen, you won't believe how it went down. He was shocked when he recognized me standing in front of that sorry assed trailer. I guess he assumed at first that I was some kind of delivery boy or something. When he opened the door and saw that it was me, he liked to shit right there and then. Remember I had just flashed my Glock at him a few hours earlier. I told him that I wasn't there to put a cap in his ass. I said I just wanted to talk. Then he gets his back up and starts hissing like a cobra, all excitable and ready to bite."

"What did you do?" asked Cletus, now spell bound by the tale.

"I up and asked him if he ever did hard time. See Cletus, the Brothers and the Arians, the Skinheads, or whatever they are calling themselves have to be able to coexist in prison. We got to be able to talk. We each have to have our own separate space in the yard. We divide up the business interests too so we can get things we need without bull shit all the time. He did two years in Raiford here in Florida. As you know, I pulled ten large in Angola over in bayou country. So we had some common ground."

"He shut his filthy trap then. Good thing too. I hadn't stowed the piece yet. I was ready to bitch slap his ass if need be. Anyway, we talk. I tell him about you, how after I got busted and thrown off the team, you were the only friend I had. I tell him straight up that I will kill him very slowly, like the Mexican Mafia do, if he messes with you at all. And I meant that, brother," Willis said solemnly.

"But, Willis, you can't do that!" Cletus said incredulously.

"I won't have to. He is truly a punk. I could see it in his eyes. He's one of those guys with a teeny pecker. I don't mean for real. That's my way of saying he got to beat his wife, slap his kids around, and bully other people to prove he's a man. Otherwise he ain't got nothing. See? A teeny pecker! He was somebody's punk ass bitch in Raiford. I'd bet a million on it Ah, I'm sorry. I know I shouldn't be using prison talk, but I don't know how else to say it."

"I understand the meaning," said Cletus. "But you are right, Willis. Keep pushing that whole experience behind you."

"But why didn't you tell me before now?" Cletus asked.

"I just wanted to be sure, Cletus. Listen man, you are damn important to me. I'd still be in the joint if it weren't for you. Outside of a few lady friends, you all I got. Anyway I watched him for a few days but he didn't come anywhere near you," Willis answered.

"Let me ask you, Willis. Is he worth trying to salvage? Could he ever be a decent husband and father?"

"Boy, are you asking the wrong guy! After I shot that fellow in Lake Charles, no one thought I was worth a dime, no one except you. So I don't want to say 'never.' But to tell you the truth, I don't think he'll change. He's got nothing! He's wearing that act like skin. But hey man, I'm forever grateful that you didn't give up on me."

"It's the children. It gets very risky when you factor children into the equation. You don't gamble with their future or their lives. Actually I think you have him pegged," said Cletus.

"By the way, you did get rid of that gun right?"

"It's in a safe place. You've been cool enough to never ask how I make a living. You know ex-cons can't get a real job. I did a big favor once to a guy in prison who was fixing to go down hard. Let's just say he's grateful. Anyway he's still paranoid, and he pays me well to look after him. It's his."

"Damn, you risked a lot carrying that thing for me. Listen, Willis, I owe you big. Thanks so much for helping me out. Call me any time. Call me if you ever lose your way. Call me if you ever lose your courage. You see, I know something about that now too."

"I hear you old friend."

They shook hands and Cletus got out. With his index finger extended he pointed at Willis, nodded affirmatively, and then switched to a thumbs up. Willis smiled through the dark tinted glass, fired up the Hemi, and roared away.

Chapter 29

Loomis and Jack finally got around to interviewing Marcus Velney. They asked him to come in, and he did. Although they didn't like it, Marcus said he would not speak to them at all unless they let his friend Ernie accompany him. If they refused he would lawyer up, and they would not get a word out of him period. He told the policemen that he had a good rationale. His friend could help him explain why his name had shown up on the Rogers-Smithson murder list.

Ernie really wanted no part of it but agreed to do it for his friend. He had a somewhat irrational fear of the police.

Ernie had been mocked and threatened long ago by an ignorant cop who held him at a traffic stop for no apparent reason. The cop had said awful things to him. He had lumped Ernie together with all men who committed sex crimes against children conveniently overlooking the obvious fact that pedophiles were not necessarily gay. Also, the pedophile's desires had less to do with sex than with power and control over their victims.

He threatened to arrest Ernie for solicitation, a charge based only on the fact that he was out driving alone at night. In sum, the cop used his authoritative position to torment Ernie, like a cat would play with a wounded mouse. When he had tired of it, he finally let Ernie limp away. Fortunately Ernie never let the experience get to him. His sunny, positive disposition pushed the incident to the far reaches of his mind. But actually walking into a police building, their turf, made him a little nervous

Loomis happened to be looking out a window when Ernie and Marcus approached the building. He called Jack over.

"Look at those queens." he said sarcastically. "That one guy is wearing a flowered shirt for crying out loud! Watch, they will be our 9:00 o'clock appointment."

"Easy big fellow. I understand that you are no fan of gays but if they are coming in to see us, try to remain objective," Jack responded.

"Hey, I think I have seen the one in that shirt before. I saw him eating lunch with Beth, the girl I'm dating now, several months ago. I think he works with the Department of Children's Services too."

"You know I have a problem with those boys. I don't get it, and I can't see it," growled Loomis.

The cops moved away from the window. Jack went down to greet them while Loomis found the meeting room, slumped in a chair, and waited.

"You must be Marcus Velney and a friend?" asked Jack as the visitors entered the lobby.

"Why, yes," answered Marcus. "This is Ernie. Ernie Langhorne."

Upstairs Jack introduced the pair to his partner. Jack noted with some concern that Loomis was still brooding.

"Let's get started," said Jack as all found chairs in a tiny interview room. Then they got down to business.

Marcus knew exactly why he was there. His hatred for Rogers-Smithson was well known. Ernie was not the only one who witnessed him explode with anger at the very mention of the name. So he admitted that he was not saddened by Darnell's death. Then he offered up something that shocked Ernie and sent the interview off on a tangent.

"I am a homosexual," Marcus offered openly. "I tried to stay firmly in the closet as they say, but Darnell pulled me out and made a display of me. I used to work for him. I was his best salesman. But, he didn't care. He ruined me. I bear scars that may never heal. I have spent years trying to climb back into that closet. But, no more! My friend here doesn't know it, but he saved my life just a few days ago. I was suicidal because I didn't want to be what I am. Ernie here has always been secure with who he is. You guys probably never even give it a thought. But I was ashamed. I hated who I was. I blamed Darnell. And yes, I did say openly to some folks that I could kill the bastard."

"Say that again," said Loomis softly, almost threatening.

"What do you mean?" Marcus asked.

"You seem to be saying it was Darnell's fault that you are gay."

Marcus looked at Loomis with great trepidation. He sensed trouble. But, things had changed rapidly in the last few days. He was no longer going to put up with crap from those who had a problem with his sexual orientation, not even a cop.

"Is it my fault that I am a homosexual? A fault. A fault of mine?" Marcus asked.

"If you want to be that way, it's fine with me," said Loomis without answering the question.

"Did you choose to be a big, red headed Black man after you were born?" replied Marcus with some fire in his gut.

"Listen, Mr. Velney. I don't want to argue with you, but...."

"But what?" snapped Marcus unintimidated by the big cop.

"You had better cool your jets my friend," offered Loomis, now beginning to let harsh opinions of gays rush to the surface.

Jack started to intervene but Marcus would have none of that.

"Listen to me and listen well," Marcus began, looking straight into eyes that were glaring at him. " I'm not going to sit here and put up with shit from you. Just a few days ago I wanted to kill myself because of self- loathing. All my life I wanted to believe that I had chosen to be gay. But I finally understood that I didn't choose anything. I was born gay. You got that? I was born gay just as you were born a rather unattractive, red headed Black man. Now you can put your homophobic BS on the back burner for a while and talk to me man to man or you can continue to voice your ignorance. If so, I want to see your captain right now!"

Loomis rose. His face was flushed with anger. He was very close to losing it like he used to do years ago on the streets of New Orleans. No one talked to him like that. Yet, this middle aged little creep just did. Fortunately, down deep, way down in his soul Loomis had heard the echoes of his long departed grandmother who had told him the same thing. A zebra does not choose nor change his stripes she would often say, urging her grandson to love himself just as he was.

Jack rose too. Without even moving in the cramped space, he put a hand on Loomis' shoulder and with the caution of dismantling a bomb, he slowly was able to calm the big man and ease him back into his seat.

The four sat there for a while, each with their own thoughts.

Loomis was shell-shocked and conflicted. He still didn't understand, really. Homosexuality just didn't make any sense. But, he had been forced to do something he had never done before, actually listen to a gay man. Further there was some truth in what he had to say.

Marcus wondered why so many men, Blacks in particular, seemed to hate gays. They, more than any other group should understand, he thought. They had to fight for their rightful place in society. But, he was beginning to believe that the Black Civil Rights Movement was for Black people only. Yet, gays and lesbians had stood side by side with the Black Panthers in the sixties when they protested and fought with police. What had happened over the years?

Jack considered the damage that Loomis had done in the interview and wondered if they could retrieve anything from it at all.

Ernie was the first to speak. "I am so proud of you, Marcus. It has only been a matter of hours since you nearly exploded with hatred for Darnell Rogers-Smithson. And now, right here, you are a different person. You have found your wheels."

"Officer Loomis," Ernie went on quietly. "You almost exploded too. I mention it because I think you came to understand where Marcus was coming from. You don't have to change your opinion of gays. The four of us will not resolve the issues here. But, if you understand the tremendous pressure that builds up in a man, like yourself, who is different from others, you will understand why

Marcus was on that list of possible suspects. He was fighting with and for himself. Thank God he was able to find peace before he acted on his hate."

"Well said," whispered Loomis. He meant it too.

"Mr. Velney, I apologize for my behavior. I interjected things into this interview that should never see the light of day."

Marcus nodded his acceptance. He was beginning to relax, and he felt good.

"I don't know about things not seeing the light of day," Ernie said. "It has been very helpful to me over the years to be honest with people. At least that's what my mother always said."

"You know, Ernie," said Loomis warming a bit, " I was just thinking about what my grandmother used to say to me all the time growing up."

"Oh?" said Ernie with a smile. "What was that?"

"Just something about a zebra and its stripes," Loomis said, knowing that the others knew exactly what he meant.

"Marcus, let me ask you a few questions," Jack said, getting back on task.

"Sure," Marcus replied. "If it's about an alibi, I'm afraid that I don't have one. I was home alone in my bed sleeping like a baby."

The interview continued along the normal lines. Shortly the cops wrapped it up and ushered their visitors out of the room.

Loomis surprised the others by stopping Marcus just as he had turned to walk away. He wanted to say something more, but the words would not come. So he offered his right hand while grasping Marcus' shoulder with his left. Marcus shook his hand and smiled. Loomis, still not knowing exactly what to say, pulled Marcus closer to him and whacked him on the back two times. Then he pushed back hurriedly, released Marcus' hand, smiled awkwardly, and walked down the hall.

Several other cops had seen the gesture. One of them couldn't wait to tell everyone that Loomis was a queer. But he thought better of it. If Loomis found out who had started the rumor, there would be hell to pay. The rat might find himself beaten to a pulp by an unknown assailant, lying on a heap of garbage in a dark alley somewhere, and he knew it.

After Ernie and Marcus got into their car, they discussed how it all went. Ernie was still amazed at how quickly Marcus had righted his own ship.

"Marcus, are you sure that you are free of self doubt?"

"I have laid down that burden. I have tossed it away. I have been carrying it on my back for many, many years. I am happy for the first time since I was a child. You saw me in there. I finally know who I am, and I am never going to fight against myself again," said Marcus enthusiastically.

"OK," Ernie replied with a grin.

"Let's see about that. I'm going to put you to a little test, Marcus," Ernie followed.

"I know several gentlemen about our age you might want to meet. Are you interested in circulating a little bit?"

"You sly fox!" said Marcus. "I appreciate the thought, Ernie, but I'm not ready for that. I want more time just getting to know myself."

Chapter 30

Several days went by but it seemed that time had not passed at all. Like prisoners serving time, Loomis and Jack plodded their way through twelve to fourteen hour days absolutely convinced that they were almost working around the clock. For the two detectives time was standing still. They were not having any fun.

They had been given help on the Rogers-Smithson case. A total of four investigators were now banging away. They had interviewed every person on the list. They had made collateral contacts with numerous associates, wives and so forth. Crime scene investigators had discovered a few shell casings in the surf but no bullet slugs that they could use. The murder weapon had not been found, and they had no hopes of ever finding it. It appeared that the person who executed Darnel simply walked the shallow surf where no footprints would be found, waited for the victim nearby, and then moved up to him after he had entered the sea and blew him to smithereens. They had nothing.

The lab results finally came in regarding the murder of Milly McCanless. They had hoped that the knife might provide some answers. The blood was that of the victim but it appeared that the killer had used gloves. Purvis had been there just before the woman died. His semen was found on the body. But, they could not prove that he wielded that knife. The prosecuting attorney wanted more evidence. In truth they didn't have the stomach to push much harder because Loomis and Jack too were now convinced that Little Dicky had not done the deed. They had nothing, and they had nothing coming.

They decided to take a break from the streets and go over everything in the two murders. The full team met in a conference room. Lieutenant Orlando led the discussion. Although the new cops were not familiar with the McCanless case, they caught up quickly as Loomis worked a white board outlining what they knew.

Their most salient point was that tenuous link, the fact that in both cases, the victims were slaughtered with a great deal of malice aforethought. It was something but could just as easily be nothing. Before they really got into it, one of the new team members, a veteran of 16 years asked if they had checked with the surrounding police agencies to see if there had been similar crimes. Jack and Loomis had indeed checked with all the neighboring police agencies large and small, including those in Alabama. The Santa Rosa County Sheriff made note of a bloody slaying several years ago but he added that the perpetrator was still in prison. None of the others had reported crimes of such violence.

"Did you inquire in Okaloosa County?" asked the same cop.

"Yes, we did," said Loomis.

"How about Walton County?"

"No, we didn't go that far east," said Loomis. "You guys keep going. I'll step out and give it a try."

The group didn't even really get started again when Loomis returned.

"Believe it or not, they had a violent personal killing near a little community called Glendale only five years ago," he said, somewhat excited. "Someone ambushed a guy named Rhyman Blotch in his front yard out in the country. He was beaten to death with a blunt instrument, probably a baseball bat. They estimate that he was struck at least twenty-five times. And get this. His genitals were beaten to a pulp post mortem. Apparently the wife and four kids were visiting with grandparents in Marianna. They will be faxing the report ASAP."

The meeting broke up for awhile as they awaited the fax. The fact that they had somewhere else to look energized and excited the cops. Several of them huddled anxiously near the machine, like a bunch of expected fathers. It really didn't take long. Jack made copies and the group reconvened. At first it was quiet in the room as each man poured over the details.

Loomis was the first to speak. "This guy was begging to meet his maker!" he said derisively.

"He does have quite a record. But why did you say that?" asked one of the other investigators.

"Read the last paragraph. His wife was not visiting her parents. She left him. She grabbed the kids and went to stay with them. He was out on bond for sexually abusing his own kids!" said Jack with disgust.

"Catch that last sentence," added Loomis. "Apparently a neighbor had previously reported that he molested one of their daughters but charges were never filed."

"What do you guys think?" asked Jack speaking to the group as a whole. "The crime is unsolved. They had little physical evidence and never found a murder weapon."

"It makes you wonder if they worked that hard," murmured Loomis, almost as an aside.

"What?" asked one of the other team members.

"We had a murder case in New Orleans years ago that didn't get a full investigation. We just went through the motions. The nod to look the other way came from on high. There was nothing said really, everyone just understood that this guy deserved to die. Believe me, it was true. The sucker had violently beaten and raped several women and one beautiful little girl. It was the child. She died as a result of her injuries. When they found this clown, he had been slaughtered. Word on the street was the father of the little girl, a hard working truck driver, had done the deed. We never even interviewed him."

The men worked on for a full hour kicking around ideas and suggestions. On the top of their to-do list was the need to get more information on the Glendale killing.

The next day, Jack and Loomis piled into an unmarked car and drove east on I10 to talk to a deputy who had worked the case. They met him at the Walton County Sheriff's office in DeFuniak Springs. He had little to add that was not in the report. Having driven for almost an hour and a half, with some degree of expectation, Jack and Loomis found themselves pressing the deputy as if he were a suspect. Finally he up and handed them something.

"Did you guys check with the Department of Children's Services," he asked casually.

"No, why?" asked Jack.

"They had the family on court ordered supervision for physical abuse. Apparently the punk wasn't getting off anymore just whipping his kids. He graduated to messing with them. The assigned caseworker, the one working with the family long term, blamed herself. The sexual abuse occurred on her watch. She ended up quitting her job in a matter of weeks. They didn't have any kids, and I knew that job was very important to her. I went hunting with her husband several times. They were fine folks, and she was one hell of a good Protective Services worker. But, she couldn't shake the guilt. They finally just up and moved to Kentucky like they just had to get away from here."

"You're not saying that you suspected her, are you?" asked Loomis.

"Hell no! She was an emotional wreck. Harold, her husband just had to get her out of the area, you know, the place where this all went down. You guys may need to get to know some of those DCS workers. Most of them bust their butts for those kids."

"What was her name?" asked Loomis.

"Ester Krekan. Ester and Harold Krekan," the deputy said.

It was quiet in the car as the two investigators drove west heading back to Pensacola. Both were mulling over the new information they received in relationship to what they already knew about the two violent murders in Pensacola.

"Jack," Loomis said, breaking the silence.

"Yea," Jack said, acknowledging his partner.

"Something just hit me. Milly McCanless had a link with the Department of Children's Services. She accidentally smothered an infant. In addition she had two other children taken from her and permanently placed with the agency. Purvis told me that. Did I mention it before?"

"I think you said something about that," Jack said. "But I hadn't put it together. I just did. You have it too, don't you?"

"Yep, all three of the damn murders are somehow tied into DCS," Loomis stated somewhat proudly. "Rogers-Smithson defended himself against child sexual abuse allegations filed by DCS after he beat the criminal rap."

"OK. OK," Jack said the implications whirling through his mind like a roulette wheel. "It could be a nut case who followed newspaper stories about child abuse, an avenging angel or vigilante. Or it could be someone who actually works for the agency. Maybe," Jack continued, "maybe there's someone in that agency who...."

"Damn Jack!" Do you really think a social worker type could actually kill like that?" Loomis asked loudly. "One was cut, one was shot, and this one was beaten to death!"

Before Jack answered, the image of Beth flashed in his mind's eye. No. He knew her to be totally sincere. He knew her to be committed to her job and to the children she was charged to serve. He could not imagine for one moment that she could ever lift a finger against another human being. Then almost as an addendum to that line of thinking, he added another consideration. Beth was a karate instructor. She had been trained at least in ways to dispatch those who would harm her. In truth she probably did know how to kill.

Then Jack finally answered Loomis. "No way. Almost all of them are women. Maybe there could be a shadow figure lurking around there. Maybe one of them has a boyfriend or husband. But come on man, what would be the motive?"

Loomis considered that question for a while, as they zipped by the Crestview exit and sped on. Alone with his thoughts, he remembered.

He remembered just how close he had come to taking justice into his own hands. He was only a heartbeat away from pulling the trigger and sending a worthless piece of garbage straight to Hell. He often wondered why he didn't do it. He easily could have gotten away with it. The crazed addict had burst into the wrong apartment. The husband wasn't there so he beat the mother senseless trying to get her to give up the drugs. But she could not help him because there were no drugs there. So he killed her. Then he eliminated the witnesses as well, one by one. Clarence, age nine. Charles, age six. Charlotte, age three.

"The motive?" Loomis finally said. "Hell to pay. Just Hell to pay."

Chapter 31

As Jack showered and dressed the next morning, he was still puzzling over the fact that the Department of Children's Services had been peripherally involved in three very different, overly violent, murder cases. The problem was simple It absolutely could have been a coincidence. If so, he, Loomis and the rest of the team would be dead in the water. They had to make something of this lead or face up to the fact that they would have to start over from scratch.

But he had something else on his mind too. He would get to see Beth again. He had called her at home the evening before to see if he could drop by her office this morning to get her take on what they had learned. If he had been totally honest with himself, he would have had to admit that the real reason for the visit was simply to be with her for a few minutes again.

He showed up at 8:00 and promised not to take up too much of her time. After they exchanged pleasantries, Jack looked her straight in the eyes.

"Beth," he said. "Please forgive me. We are snowed under right now. I don't know when I can get away. You know, for our little, ah, reunion. I promise that I will come storming after you, the first opportunity I have, and you can take that to the bank."

"Too busy for me, huh?" Beth teased. "I understand Jack, I really do. There will be times that I will be all wrapped up in cases too. Don't take too long though."

"Whoa!" Jack laughed. "We could just clean off the top of your desk...."

"I can wait," Beth replied with a pout that seemed to mean the exact opposite of what she just said. The look forced Jack to pause to make sure he read her correctly. He assumed that she had meant what she said.

"All right then," Jack said with a smile. "We had better get down to business. I'm here for some help. We are looking at three unsolved murder cases, two recent and one several years back. They were all rather brutal slayings. Also, there is a link but a tenuous one at that. DCS is the link. You guys were involved with all the murder victims in one way or another."

After Beth took in what he had said, she asked for more details. Jack provided a sketch of each case

"Let's see," Beth said. "I'm familiar with Rogers-Smithson and Milly McCanless. But I never heard of anyone named Rhyman Blotch."

"That man was murdered in Walton County. Your turf doesn't extend that far to the east does it?" asked Jack.

"Why yes it does," said Beth. "Our area takes in Walton County, and we have an office in Defuniak Springs. Maybe you need to speak to our Area Supervisor, Marlon Munch."

"Look, I think you guys on the line would be of more help," said Jack. "I guess what I need is some information on the Protective Services workers who were assigned to the two cases here. I already know the worker who was responsible for the family in Defuniak."

"Do you know who handled the two cases from this county?" asked Jack.

"Eleanor Porter investigated both of those cases," Beth said with emphasis on the word "investigated." "But remember Jack this unit is not responsible for on-going supervision. The protective services caseworkers handle that."

"OK. I got that, I think," Jack responded.

"We never got a thing on Rogers-Smithson," Beth continued. "He was found not guilty in criminal court and the sexual abuse case against him was dropped. There was no caseworker assigned for supervision."

"The other one should be easy enough. I can pull that for you off our case information system."

With that, Beth turned and started typing on her keyboard. In a matter of minutes she had the name of the protective services worker previously assigned to Millie McCanless.

"Dawn Weygant," Beth said. "But now you have another problem. She quit three years ago. Her husband was stationed here at Corry Field for a while and then he was transferred"

"Man," Jack said. "I was hoping to get a break. We became interested in the Defuniak case because the worker assigned to supervise the family before the sexual abuse took place was apparently devastated, like it was all her fault. She and her husband left town shortly thereafter."

"Do you suspect that worker? Or, her husband, maybe?"

"Her husband would have had a good motive for that slaying. The woman was really broken up by all that went down. Everyone who knew her said she wasn't capable," Jack responded.

"We were hoping to tie all three of these cases together. But, from what you have told me, I don't think there is any link to the two murders here. We may have to start over."

"If you think about it Jack, there may be a certain logic to why the agency would have ties with three people who were victims of murder, particularly over a span of several years. They all hurt children. Basically they were unsavory characters and probably had a dark side. It could be as simple as that. Their deaths may have more to do with drug dealing or other criminal activity. I'm sorry, Jack," Beth said in conclusion. "Is there anything else we could do for you?"

"Just ask around a little," replied Jack. "Maybe something useful will come up. If nothing else, we may be able to get some leads on the Rhyman Blotch case for the Sheriff's people in Defuniak Springs."

"Let's go ask Cletus and Ernie about this while you are here," Beth suggested.

Jack and Beth walked down the hall and found the two huddled over a pile of paper on Cletus's desk. Beth excused herself for interrupting them and introduced her friend.

"So good to see you again," gushed Ernie with genuine delight.

"Well, Ernie," replied Jack, " we meet twice in a matter of days. It's good to see you again too. You really helped us the other day in more ways than one."

"You are too kind, Inspector Mulkey. I just considered that exchange as our civic duty."

"What can we do for you?" asked Cletus cheerfully, wondering to himself if Jack might be gay.

"I need some information concerning a Walton County staffer. I'm looking for anyone who knew Ester Krekan, a protective service worker. The father of two small children apparently had sexually abused both of them. Unfortunately the court had already placed the family under her supervision for physical child abuse. Am I saying this right?"

"Sure," Cletus answered. "You're on track."

"Anyway," Jack went on. "This guy was murdered after getting out on bond. It was never solved. And that case might have something to do with…"

"I remember her," Ernie shot out excitedly. "She was so nice. I bumped into her at an area meeting. I think it was about the use of volunteers. I was so sad when I heard what happened to her."

"What did happen to her, Ernie?" asked Jack.

"She had a break down, a mental breakdown," Ernie said quietly, repeating what Jack already knew. "She was placed in a mental health facility for a short time as a result of a suicide attempt. Within weeks she and her husband moved out of state, I believe."

"Yea, the brass crucified her!" Cletus said with feeling.

"I forgot her name," Cletus continued. "Everybody was talking about that case at the time. We sure heard about it at the supervisory level. Headquarters staff poured into Defuniak Springs and completed a review of her work. I think they were camped out over there for almost a week. They found one single breach of the contact requirements and basically threw her under the bus. You see, Jack, if something bad happens to a dependent child who was referred to our agency, someone has to pay. This gal almost paid with her life."

"I remember all that now too, Jack," mused Beth quietly. "It's sad that I forgot her name as well. By all accounts she was an excellent worker. She was well liked and respected in that town. I don't like to think that she was just tossed aside and forgotten, but I guess she was."

"It sounds to me like lots of folks will remember her, given a little memory jog," said Jack. "If you guys could just put the word out that we are interested in talking to anyone who knew her and her husband, something may come up. I'm thinking there might be one little piece of this puzzle out there that may help us."

Jack thanked them all and strode to his car without the usual kick in his step. In his gut he still wanted to believe that the link with DCS was something, if not the key to solving the crimes. But up in his head where logic prevailed, he was just about convinced that there was nothing to it. Beth's point that DCS would be involved with a number of families involving unsavory characters who might end up dead seemed plausible.

Even the over use of violence didn't necessarily mean there was a link, he thought. Violent murder was no longer a rarity in our society as a whole. In bigger cities and even in some rural areas, over kill was the method of choice often used to wipe out anyone who dared to offend the killer, on purpose or not. Cases of murder abounded of those shot several times for nothing more than a sideward glance or for the loose change in their pockets. Life was getting very cheap out there, he concluded.

Later that afternoon, after taking two calls from DCS workers from Walton County that added little to the investigation, Jack received a third.

"Hi," the caller said. "I have information for you concerning that case in Defuniak Springs. I can't make it in right now, as I will be very busy. Can I meet you at your office tomorrow afternoon at 4:00?"

"Sure," said Jack. "Can you give me your..."

Click.

Chapter 32

When Jack found Loomis and told him that he had someone coming in for an interview, Loomis' eyes lit up. He too was growing pessimistic and something as tangible as an interview gave him some hope. Police work can drain the individual cop. It is not uncommon for officers to transfer every once in a while for a change of scenery. Loomis loved being an investigator, but even he had been considering a transfer, maybe work the streets again as a uniform patrolman.

The two were supposed to be off that afternoon, but they hung around after a late lunch and waited. At almost precisely 4:00 P.M. a woman walked into the building. Jack and Loomis were at their perch at the second floor window. They both saw her but took no notice. They both looked through her, looked past her. She disappeared below them at the main entrance. A few minutes later another policeman brought her to them as she had been asking for Jack Mulkey. She confirmed that she was the one who had called the day before. Following introductions the three took chairs in an interview room.

Once settled, Jack thanked her for coming in.

"Oh, I hope that I can help. Maybe I can share some insight into this tragedy."

After more pleasantries, Jack gave her a few details concerning their interest and asked her what she knew.

"Well, I remember that case because it really caused a stir over there. The sexual abuse was bad enough. On top of that our central office decided to make someone responsible, to manufacture a fall guy. They centered in on Ester Krekan, an excellent protective services worker. Some of the members of the community came to her defense, including the judges, but the die was cast. You could almost say they took a mug shot of her and proudly announced that she had abused those poor children."

"So you knew Ester?" Jack asked.

"Yes, I knew her. She was committed to her job, a hard worker. More importantly, she was a fine person, sweet and kind. Maybe child welfare was not the place for her."

"Why do you say that?" Jack followed.

"She wasn't tough enough at the core. See Officer Mulkey, our work, like yours I'm sure, can get to you. I guess you could say she was lost in the heat of the battle. She didn't know how to defend herself. Some would call it combat fatigue although I surely don't want to imply that it is as bad as all that."

"We knew that she took the fall for the sexual abuse of the two little girls," Loomis interjected, rather impatiently.

"Yes, she did, Officer Loomis. As I said, she just seemed to be exhausted by it all. She wasn't strong enough."

"So, there's no way she could have murdered Mr. Blotch?" Loomis went on, pushing a little.

"Hardly. She was in no condition to do anything much."

"What about her husband?" Jack asked.

"I didn't know him well. I only met him once. He was a gentle sort, a good man. I was told he was a leader in his church. That's not to imply that he was soft or something. To the contrary, he was a man's man of sorts, into hunting, fishing and the like. But in my opinion he was not capable of murder."

Loomis started to squirm in his seat. He had heard all this before. There seemed to be nothing new here, and he was already getting frustrated.

"Listen," Loomis blurted out. "We are trying to figure out who might have killed Rhyman Blotch. That's our bottom line. Do you have any idea who might have wanted to beat him to death?"

"I thought you wanted to know about Ester?"

"Yes," said Loomis wearily, "but in relationship to the murder."

"Well, there is no way she could have done it, and I don't believe her husband was interested in revenge."

"What made you mention revenge," asked Loomis, trying desperately to find some new ground.

"Well, she attempted suicide and had to be held for an evaluation. I'm sure he was upset that his wife tried to kill herself. I guess he could have blamed Rhyman Blotch for the whole thing. Let's face it, if not for Blotch, Ester would still be there helping children and their families in Defuniak Springs."

"Look, sexual abuse of children is as bad as it can get," Loomis stated flatly. "But taking another life is an extreme as well, isn't it? Blotch would have gone to prison for decades. Why not let justice run its course. What more could the killer have wanted?"

"Well, there are different ways to kill someone. Ester didn't have a chance after he was done with her."

The cops exchanged a glance in the split second following the answer to the last question. Both had noticed that their interviewee had just implied that Blotch had done something to Ester Krekan, something personal, something that hurt her. They wondered about the implication and their interest level began to rise. Like lions spotting an Impala with a slight limp, their enthusiasm and interest suddenly peaked.

"Are you sure about her husband? If Blotch had hurt his wife, he would have to be a prime suspect, right?" asked Loomis.

"I don't think so. He was not unlike Ester. Even though he was all man and enjoyed hunting, fishing and the like, he had a delightful easy-going personality."

"But Botch had really hurt his wife, right?" Jack continued.

"Yes, he did. That man was a beast. He trampled all over his wife and kids and everyone else he came into contact with."

"Including his own family, neighbors, Mr. and Mrs. Krekan, anyone, right?" Jack asked.

"Yes, most definitely. You see officers people like Rhyman Blotch simply infect the world with their poison, spreading their own particular brand about like radioactive waste. Certainly you have known people like that. They literally infect the air we breathe."

"Bottom line then, who could have done this if not the Krekans? Who would want to destroy him like that?" Loomis asked.

"I'm not sure. I guess you two will have to figure that out. All I know is that I'm happy the man is dead. Did you ever feel that way about a murderer, Officer Loomis?"

Again, the cops paused, a few hairs bristling on the back of their necks. This time it was the question. "Did you ever feel that way about a murderer?" Rhyman Blotch had not murdered anyone. The person with them in the small interview room was using strong language to describe this man, perhaps revealing feelings bordering on hatred and disgust.

Both men seized the moment with a degree of confusion. Loomis couldn't fathom why this sweet coworker was talking this way. Jack was literally fidgeting in his chair trying to understand. He knew this woman. At least he thought he did, and her tone was surprising to say the least.

As usual, Loomis went straight to the point, "Why did you call Rhyman Blotch a murderer?" he asked.

"That's funny coming from you guys. You seem to be missing the bigger picture. We work with child abusers, people who neglect, abandon, and hurt their children. Those crimes have a far-reaching impact. Victims dry up and fade away. Mothers, often battered themselves, die over and over again. This man needed..."

"Needed what?" Jack asked quietly.

"Killing. Some people need killing!"

"And...?" Jack prodded ever so gently with a voice just above a whisper.

"Is your recording equipment turned on?" the visitor said.

"No, but I'll see to it," answered Jack, already on his feet and moving.

"Officer Loomis, I think you should advise me of my rights too."

"Ahh, sure," answered Loomis, belatedly, in a state of confusion. He then produced a form from a legal sized notebook he was carrying and began reading the standard text. When he was finished with the procedure, a signature was secured on the form, and they moved on.

Both Jack and Loomis could hardly contain their enthusiasm. Loomis felt his heart race a little, and he had to sit still a bit to let it calm. Jack came back into the room breathing hard, like he had just run a mile or two. He began to inhale and exhale deeply like an expectant mother, breathing to relax. There was no way for them to hide their excitement. They knew that they were about to solve one murder case and possibly three. The implication was almost staggering.

Once Jack was settled again, the interview began in earnest.

"What can you tell us?" Jack asked very simply. And never in his career would he ever get a response as surprising as he did right there and then.

"Let's cut to the chase," said their guest. "I killed Rhyman Blotch, Milly McCanless and Darnell Rogers-Smithson."

"Really?" Loomis said, almost in disbelief, like someone had told him he won the lottery.

"You just up and whacked all three of them?" he asked, bluntly.

A simple affirmative was the reply. Both Jack and Loomis froze for an instant. It was too much. Eleanor Porter? Three murders? Just like that?

Jack was the first to regain his composure. "Can you tell us why?" he asked.

"Have you ever watched one of those nature documentaries?" she replied. "You know, where the cheetah cubs are about to be attacked by hyenas or the baby rhino is surrounded by lions?"

"Yea, I guess?" Jack said puzzled.

"Well, do you remember wondering why the cameraman and the crew didn't intervene to stop the slaughter? I always wanted them to rescue the baby, but they never did. They felt like they couldn't alter things, that nature just had to run its course. I guess after watching so many children getting hurt, I decided to intervene.

Both men sat absolutely still again, contemplating her words. She had used a great analogy, and it actually made a great deal of sense.

After a few moments, Loomis spoke. "Tell us about the first one, Rhyman Blotch?" he asked. As soon as he let the words out, he wondered if there could be more than three.

"Ester Krekan was a dear friend of mine, much like a sister. I had known her for several years. She was a wonderful person. She was younger than me, but I found that I could talk with her like no other. I shared my hopes and fears. I was married years ago and was very happy. I became pregnant and lost my little girl prematurely. I stopped being a mother and a wife immediately. Ester was childless. She could not conceive. She and I saw much of ourselves in one another. I guess you could say we held each other very close. For certain I have not recovered from her death."

"So she is dead then?" Jack asked.

"Mr. Blotch killed her. No, he didn't actually touch her. But, he killed her nevertheless."

"Can you imagine what happens to a little girl when a man forces himself into her body? It's not talk for polite society, is it? But the truth is worse than you can imagine. I happen to know that from personal experience. But, I digress. As far as I know, both of those little girls are still suffering from the initial rape and from continued assault over a few weeks until the awful abuse came to light. They were not only traumatized beyond belief, they needed medical attention for rips and tears to very sensitive tissue, and not just the vagina either."

Jack and Loomis sat spell bound. Eleanor Porter's confession was not only real, it was chilling. It struck them like the icy winds of winter. Her brief description of child sexual abuse went way beyond mere words. Images flooded their minds in intense color and clarity. The pictures froze them in their tracks, gripping both veterans of murder and mayhem like nothing they had seen inside the yellow tape before. They were uncomfortable. They wanted air. But, they knew that Eleanor Porter was not going to let them escape the madness any more than she could herself.

"Ester blamed herself," Eleanor continued. "How else does one deal with such horror? You no doubt know that she was treated briefly in Defuniak Springs for a suicide attempt. You may not know that she was successful at it eight months later. I didn't even wait for that. As soon as I heard he was out on bond, I purchased an aluminum baseball bat, lured him outside by making noises and then bashed him to Hell, where he belonged. To me it was no more than killing a rattlesnake with a garden hoe."

"Milly McCanless was an addict and a prostitute. But she could get pregnant at the drop of a hat. An old record indicated that she had three children before I got involved. One ran away and was never heard from again. The other two were just handed out to relatives like puppies or something. Even she didn't know where they were. I never could find them."

"When I made my initial investigation, she had had four more children by different men. The first, a little boy, was born prematurely addicted to cocaine. He died a few hours later, unable to deal with the poison raging through his system. The middle two were victims of fetal alcohol syndrome. We got then out of that place and severed her parental rights. They probably will never be adopted as they both exhibit severe learning and behavior problems. The last was smothered in the landfill where Milly lived. All that was missing were the sea gulls. She ran through her life like a huge rat along with many of the more common variety in her own excrement and trash. She got drunk one night and rolled her bulk on top of her baby and never even heard the cries or whimpers. When that baby was found, the little body was crushed and even veteran cops like you guys had tears in their eyes."

"When I found out later that she had an eighth child, a little girl, I dropped by to see her. It was not an official visit. I just wanted to see how she was doing. Nothing had changed. Basically she might as well have spit in my face. She was drunk when she answered the door, and she admitted proudly that she got high at every opportunity. I feared that that baby would die there too."

"I took a good butcher knife out of my kitchen drawer and stalked her until the time was right. I entered her house and slit her throat. It was easy. You just let the blade do the work for you, like cutting a watermelon. I was worried about the fact that I had been involved with her before, so I set up one of her Johns to take the fall. According to the newspaper you fellows already know that I took the baby to Atmore and called 911. I hope that child is free of fetal alcohol syndrome. Do either of you know?" she asked.

The question jarred the cops for a moment. Jack and Loomis were still trying to wrap their heads around what they had been hearing. Neither had ever heard a confession like this. Both had seen tough guys break down and cry trying to explain what they had done and why. But, Eleanor Porter was simply telling them how it all went down with no hesitation and no sign of remorse. Loomis began to feel some compassion for her, like a now fallen champion for child victims, an avenging angel sent by God to destroy the wicked. Jack marveled at her absolute strength of conviction all packaged in a very strong woman, grey hair, slight limp, and all.

Back to the here and now, still figuratively blinking like they had been pushed out of the shadows, both Jack and Loomis paused hoping the other would answer her question. They didn't know about the child. Should they? Why did she ask them anyway? The answers escaped them, but a slight feeling of guilt did not.

Finally Loomis simply told her that he didn't know.

"I shot Darnell in his face," Eleanor said flatly, abruptly moving on. "I had begun to dream of that smirk he displayed in court after his lawyers had worked their magic. Years ago I picked up a hand gun for protection. I live alone you know. The guy who waited on me recommended a Glock with hollow-point ammunition. He said it would bring down any one who bothered me. I guess that smirk really did aggravate me. I literally enjoyed wiping that creepy smile off his ugly mug. I want you to know that I would do it all over again in a heartbeat. I credit myself for removing that man from the face of the earth. He can't hurt anyone else any more."

"I guess you can understand at some level how it must have felt as his victim. She knew well enough that he had raped her. Yet he was declared innocent all the way around. How does a teen justify that? She was really struggling with the rape, with depression. There was some doubt that she would be able to make it. So I helped her. I put her rapist on the medical examiner's slab. I put his sorry butt into his perfectly gorgeous silk lined, tightly closed casket. I sent him to his grave where he can slowly rot and decay. She's a tough one, that girl. She will be OK. Killing her rapist was probably great therapy for her, wouldn't you agree?"

Loomis responded again, "I think we have some agreement on that, although I probably should not say so with a video tape running. I can tell you one thing, Miss Porter. You can never justify taking another's life. But hey, you have come very close to doing just that today."

The three went on for a long time. Finally Loomis left to secure an arrest warrant leaving Jack and Eleanor alone.

"Why did you turn yourself in?" Jack asked. "We may not have found you, you know."

"Call it my retirement, Jack. I need to get away," she said smiling, like her words amused her. "Well, that didn't sound right, did it? I'm not going anywhere, "she said smiling.

"Anyway what I meant to say is that I am very tired. I have been at it for almost 38 years. That's a very long time in combat, don't you think. I have lots of wounds, lots of experiences like the ones I talked about today. Obviously I am troubled. I can't go around just killing people. I want to find peace before I die. I want to be able to see some of the goodness in man that I have lost sight of over these many years. Even if I get the death penalty, I should have plenty of time to read and study."

"If they let me, I'd like to work with my fellow prisoners too, at least those who will be going home some day. I think I have a lot to offer women who find themselves in trouble. I honestly think I may be able to help."

"There's one more thing. I want to write a book. I want to tell my story. There may be something in my experiences that will promote more public awareness and understanding of child abuse and neglect. I don't know why, but we tend to work out of the public view until something goes wrong. Then, like a coalmine accident, we bury those staffers who were caught up in the tragedy and keep operating without really correcting the safety violations. Like some state and federal regulatory agencies, we seem to exist solely as a shell with a false front. The public can see that we are there. We exist. Therefore the problem is solved. Just send the little hummers to DCS. But we are never really given the power, political support and muscle needed to do the job right."

Jack listened very carefully to Eleanor Porter. He had someone very important to him in the same line of work. He silently vowed to be a rock for Beth should she find herself adrift in the sea of human misery.

When Loomis returned, Eleanor was formally arrested and transferred to jail. Her retirement had begun in earnest.

Chapter 33

It was after 10:00 P.M. by the time Jack was able to phone Beth. The arrest of Eleanor Porter stirred up a hornets' nest of activity. Word spread like wildfire. All the brass wanted first hand information. All the major players associated with the three murder cases outside of the Sheriff's Department had to be informed. There were several briefings and in-house meetings to attend. Finally, Jack and Loomis had to complete a mound of paper work, including that necessary to free one little bastard named Purvis Dickie who was as innocent as the day is long.

The Sheriff understood that the story would be big news in New York or Chicago let alone Pensacola. How often does a little old lady, a social worker no less, kill a man with a baseball bat? The press would soon bombard them, and he knew that he needed to get ahead of the game, so every member of his command staff was called in to help coordinate publicity.

He wanted a press release prepared and press conferences set up ASAP. Thus, assignments were fired around like bullets from a machine gun. Jack and Loomis had to be ensconced in the main conference room for over an hour simply to be available to any in-house staffer who needed information to complete those assignments. During a lull after the local press briefing that both Jack and Loomis attended, Jack was able to slip away to make his call.

"Beth," Jack said. "I want you to hear this from me. We arrested Eleanor Porter this afternoon for the three homicides."

"What!" Beth said in disbelief.

"It's true, Beth. She walked in here and gave a full confession. She knew details, and she explained everything."

"She has to be making it up," Beth surmised. "She has been ill lately. Maybe it's her medication..."

"Beth! Beth!" Jack said with some urgency. "You are not listening to me. Eleanor killed those three people."

Now, Jack was greeted with silence. He knew she was still there, her mind searching for answers that would not come. He waited.

"Jack," she said very quietly, almost in a whisper. "When can I see you?"

"I may be here all night. I'll see if the Sheriff can spare me tomorrow morning early. There's another press conference scheduled for 10:00 for national media. I'll tell him that you folks need help in coming to grips with this. He's solid Beth, and I think he will understand. Call Cletus. Tell him what happened. Maybe he should alert the others so they don't have to hear it in the news or something. Tell him that we may come by first thing in the morning. I think you guys will need to wrestle with this and maybe we can help."

With the full weight of a tragedy bearing down on her, she called Cletus. He offered to help her reach the others but she refused. She wanted to make those calls herself. She asked him to alert the other unit supervisors and anyone else he thought should know. Next she called her friends, her coworkers: Shanice. Vickie. Bill. Ernie. Talking it through with her friends served to help her keep the grief in place. She would have trouble going to sleep that night, but she would eventually drift off, aware of the pain but a little closer to recovery.

The Sheriff had no problem with a break for Jack in the morning as long as he was back in plenty of time for the next news conference at 10:00. Jack grabbed Loomis and asked him if he wanted to go to DCS with him.

"Get me out of here, Mulk," said Loomis. "This place is like a riot, confusing, loud and dangerous. But I don't know if I can help you with those folks. Think about it, one of their own is a serial killer."

"You've known rogue cops haven't you? You have seen some of the boys in blue cross the line. I think you have more to offer than you think," stated Jack. "Think about it partner."

When the two investigators arrived, all hands were on deck. Ernie, who had been waiting for them at the main entrance of the building, led them into a witness room by the two courtrooms where the unit sat rather quietly around a large table. Their small numbers made them seem lost in there and in fact most of them were. The usual banter was gone. No one felt like making small talk.

Jack walked by Beth, leaned down, and said a few quiet words to her before he found a seat at the end of the table. She looked up at him and gave him a weak but tender smile.

Cletus welcomed the police, and he was truly glad that they had come. The group hadn't even mentioned Eleanor's name let alone begun to grapple with the how and whys. Once the guests were introduced and seated, Cletus took initiative. He expressed his own shock. He discussed his grief for Eleanor and finally his own regrets as a supervisor that he had not been able to help her in some way. Then he asked Jack and Loomis to say a few words.

Jack stood and spoke, "I was talking with my partner here on the way over. We have a lot in common with you. We walk the mean streets and occasionally the pressure builds. I want you to listen to my partner. He has twenty-two years under his belt as a cop. He worked for twenty of those years in New Orleans and Memphis, Tennessee; cities that make Pensacola look like a quaint New England village in comparison. He knows what happened to Eleanor, and I think he can help you come to grips with her fate."

Loomis rose laboriously as all eyes turned to him.

"I'll get straight to the point," Loomis said.

"What can you do emotionally or otherwise when you run into people that do horrible things to children? Occasionally we get to shoot felons and other bastards who break the law. You might be surprised how good that feels. If nothing else we often get to cuff them and put them behind bars even if it is only for a night or two. There's satisfaction in that as well. More importantly, we then move on. You guys can't shoot any body. You can't put them in jail either. You guys, at least with the rest of your outfit, are stuck with them until the children are taken care of somehow."

"On top of that we are often called heroes because we hang our butts out in defense of the public. Sure many cops get killed or injured in the line of duty. Good hard working cops are heroes for the sacrifices they make. But I have never heard anyone call you folks heroes no matter what you do. In truth most people don't know or care if you are walking those mean streets or not."

"I think the common perception of you is totally wrong. I know because I had it wrong too, that is before I met Eleanor Porter."

"I don't know her very well, but she is one tough SOB. I felt a kinship with her as she talked. She can be a sister of mine. She rose up in defense of defenseless children and struck with a swift and mighty hand. That was wrong on all counts. For sure! But, I am almost proud of her. I share her power. I share her guts. Jack and I arrested her and put her behind bars for the rest of her life. But we damn sure understand, and we damn sure will not condemn her," Loomis said, almost in a rant, each word punctuated with greater volume and greater feeling.

Loomis had to pause for a few seconds after that. It seemed that the speech had taken him to an emotional level that normally lay hidden under his cop cool and calm.

Then he summed it up. "When Eleanor spoke with us, she was not remorseful. She knew exactly what she had done and why. She whacked some bad people. So what? Even that does not erase decades of dedicated service to kids. If you must grieve for her loss, do so. Then get over it. But whatever you do, do not abandon her. Do not feel sorry for her. She has not died. She is very much alive, and her head is held high."

"She told Jack and I that she views prison as retirement of sorts. She will be busy there helping other inmates and writing a book about social work and what you do. That gal is going to stay at it until she dies. She's just changing the venue."

"Feel her strength! Feel her passion. You have an extremely important job to do. I shouldn't say it, this way, but get off your ass and get back at it ASAP. There are still thousands of kids out there that need you."

Without flourish or a thank you, Loomis just sat down. There was stunned silence in the room. Eleanor's closest friends did not expect THAT. The big hulking cop who had arrested her did not see her violent crimes as an end, but only as a new beginning.

Finally Jack stood again and asked if anyone had any questions. He knew that it was like asking the same thing of a group who had just watched an autopsy. They might need a moment to catch their breath. Silence from the group proved the point.

"Well, we have to get back. There is a major press conference scheduled for 10:00. I sincerely hope that losing one of your own like this will not distract you from your work for long. You guys are needed out there. Thanks for allowing us to drop by."

Cletus thanked the cops and gave each a warm shake of the hand. Beth smiled and nodded to Jack approvingly as he and his partner headed to the door. Otherwise, there were no pleasant exchanges between cops and social workers as they left.

Once the two men were gone, the remaining members of the now once more depleted child abuse and neglect investigations unit, supervised by one Cletus Jones, simply sat alone with their thoughts. A deafening silence gripped the room like the eerie quiet of a battlefield after the blood had been shed. The group sat still breathing an air of uncertainty.

Finally Beth spoke. "Let's face it. No matter how hard we try, children still get hurt. It's obvious that Eleanor saw way too much pain over the years. I just spoke with her the other day. It's probably obvious by now, but I have a new love in my life. I went to her because I was worried about sharing a commitment that I already have, a commitment to this job."

"El had no one for years. It is painfully obvious now, but she warned me not to do the same. She actually said it could be dangerous. And it was. See, we need friends. We need family. We must be whole and well grounded before we can truly give to others."

"Let's not forget Eleanor. She has been too important to each and every one of us. But, let's not make her a hero. More importantly, let's not become like her either."

"Shanice, since we took on Leonard Samford I feel like your sister, and I want that relationship to continue. Bill, Vickie, if you two don't keep us laughing, we will have to find others who will. Ernie, keep the compliments and the smiles coming. We need that. Boy, do we need that! Cletus, we will need to replace you. You are nothing but a pain in the ass," she said.

That last comment, so totally out of character for Beth brought peels of laughter from everyone, especially Mr. Jones. They all giggled until they got silly. As they always seemed to do, they managed to put things in prospective and then they moved on.

Soon they were at their appointed places, back at it again.

Beth sat quietly for a moment at her desk before she started making phone calls, thinking. She was truly ready to have some fun, now and for the rest of her life, and she knew exactly where to find it.

Chapter 34

Several days went by and things began to return to normal. Both Jack and Loomis got a few days off. Loomis was headed to Brownsville to visit a very close friend. They had discovered that they both liked chess. They sharpened up their games by playing for hours after the bar closed. The winner got to decide what games they would play next.

Jack called Beth and set up a date. After they agreed on a time and a place to devote themselves to becoming the beast with two backs, the conversation turned a bit risqué. Both ended up squirming a little in their chairs, warming to the idea. Although they did not say it, they both would have jumped into a car and left immediately if they could.

A fellow policeman had told Jack of a place in rural Santa Rosa County, a place called the Love Nest. For $350 a honeymoon couple, or others who just wanted to run through the Karma Sutra, could book an isolated bungalow for two nights. The place was equipped with everything the couple would need including food, beverages, satellite radio/TV, hot tub, king sized bed, mirrors and a few sex toys, new in the box. Once booked the couple was given codes for two separate combination locks that secured gates protecting the two-mile road in and out. Once there they would not see another living soul until they left, as their privacy was assured.

At the appointed hour Jack picked up Beth at her apartment in his Jeep Cherokee. She greeted him at the door sporting a fiery red sundress that did everything imaginable to accent her natural beauty and curvaceous body. Jack was floored. There she was, the woman who had been hiding her light under a basket for many years, dressed to kill. If he had not already made his deposit for the Love Nest, he would have never bothered to leave her apartment. Beth playfully handed him a tiny overnight bag and winked. The message, easily discerned by her would-be lover, was simple. Beth wouldn't need a lot of clothes for the next two days.

They found the cut off road and ventured along a canopied lane out into the woods. At the first fence line, Jack bounded out, popped the combination lock, and swung open the gate. When he jumped back into the Jeep, he could not help but notice that Beth was sitting with her back against the passenger door, looking directly across at him, one leg pulled up with her on the seat, the other splayed out to the floor. The sundress continued to protect her modesty, but only. She was twirling something on her finger and smiling impishly at him. Because of the fading light, he could not make out what it was. Then it hit him. Beth had peeled off a pair of black panties.

Jack paused for a split second to turn off the engine. Then he lunged at her. But Beth, anticipating the move, squirmed free opened her door and got out. He soon followed. For a minute or two they played tag. Jack tried very hard to tag her in more ways than one. But Beth, not Jack, was nimble and quick. She laughed as she led him on a merry chase encircling the Jeep, back and forth, round and round.

A doe with two yearlings listened nervously from a far, adjacent field. The noise coming from the road in the distance was strange and unlike anything she had experienced. She almost fled when she heard particularly loud peels of laughter. She stood alert, her tail raised, ears twitching She decided there was no threat and returned to feed once more as the raucous sounds abated. All the doe could hear was a soft, rhythmic mechanical sound which was less threatening, so she relaxed.

Then slowly at first, still in rhythm, came low registered gasps and moans. Soon thereafter and with much more urgency, loud guttural animal noises crescendoed through the field.

All three deer bolted as one.

Beth and Jack were premature.

They hadn't even made it to their Love Nest.

LaVergne, TN USA
30 December 2010
210662LV00004B/3/P